PRAISE FOR TAMMY L. GRACE

"*A Season of Hope* is a perfect holiday read! Warm wonderful and gentle tale reflecting small town romance at its best."
— *Jeanie, review of A Season for Hope: A Christmas Novella*
"This book is a clean, simple romance with a background story very similar to the works of Debbie Macomber. If you like Macomber's books you will like this one. The main character, Hope and her son Jake are on a road trip when their car breaks down, thus starts the story. A holiday tale filled with dogs, holiday fun, and the joy of giving will warm your heart.
— *Avid Mystery Reader, review of A Season for Hope: A Christmas Novella*
"This book was just as enchanting as the others. Hardships with the love of a special group of friends. I recommend the series as a must read. I loved every exciting moment. A new author for me. She's fabulous."
—*Maggie!, review of Pieces of Home: A Hometown Harbor Novel (Book 4)*
"Tammy is an amazing author, she reminds me of Debbie Macomber… Delightful, heartwarming...just down to earth."

— *Plee, review of A Promise of Home: A Hometown Harbor Novel (Book 3)*

"This was an entertaining and relaxing novel. Tammy Grace has a simple yet compelling way of drawing the reader into the lives of her characters. It was a pleasure to read a story that didn't rely on theatrical tricks, unrealistic events or steamy sex scenes to fill up the pages. Her characters and plot were strong enough to hold the reader's interest."

—*MrsQ125, review of Finding Home: A Hometown Harbor Novel (Book 1)*

"This is a beautifully written story of loss, grief, forgiveness and healing. I believe anyone could relate to the situations and feelings represented here. This is a read that will stay with you long after you've completed the book."

—*Cassidy Hop, review of Finally Home: A Hometown Harbor Novel (Book 5)*

Killer Music and Deadly Connection are award-winning novels, earning the 2016 & 2017 Mystery Gold Medal by the Global E-Book Awards

"Killer Music is a clever and well-crafted whodunit. The vivid and colorful characters shine as the author gradually reveals their hidden secrets—an absorbing page-turning read."

— *Jason Deas, bestselling author of Pushed and Birdsongs*

"I could not put this book down! It was so well written & a suspenseful read! This is definitely a 5-star story! I'm hoping there will be a sequel!"

—*Colleen, review of Killer Music*

"This is the best book yet by this author. The plot was well crafted with an unanticipated ending. I like to try to leap ahead and see if I can accurately guess the outcome. I was able to predict some of the plot but not the actual details which made reading the last several chapters quite engrossing."

—*0001PW, review of Deadly Connection*

A SEASON FOR HOPE

CHRISTMAS IN SILVER FALLS BOOK 1

TAMMY L. GRACE

LONE MOUNTAIN PRESS

A Season for Hope
A Christmas novella by
Tammy L. Grace

www.tammylgrace.com
Facebook: https://www.facebook.com/tammylgrace.books
Twitter: @TammyLGrace
Instagram: @authortammylgrace

Published in the United States by Lone Mountain Press, Nevada

ISBN 978-1-945591-08-2 (eBook)
ISBN 978-1-945591-20-4 (paperback)
FIRST EDITION
Printed in the United States of America

ALSO BY TAMMY L. GRACE

Tammy would love to connect with readers on social media and her website at www.tammylgrace.com. Remember to subscribe to her mailing list and you'll receive the fun interview she did with the dogs from her Hometown Harbor Series as an exclusive free gift only available to her subscribers. **Subscribe here: https:// wp.me/P9umIy-e**

Follow Tammy on Facebook and click over and follow Tammy on BookBub and Amazon by clicking the follow buttons on her pages.

With warm Christmas wishes, from my family to yours

A SEASON FOR HOPE

CHRISTMAS IN SILVER FALLS

Book 1

1

_____

The car sputtered and clunked as it let out its last breath. Abby sighed and took off her glove so she could grip the key in the ignition. She put her foot on the gas and gave the cool metal a firm twist. The engine cranked, and she smiled and put it in gear. The spark of relief she experienced was snuffed when the car wouldn't budge and died again.

She plucked her cell phone from her purse and glanced at the sleeping boy in the passenger seat. Thankful she had service, she located a tow truck service and put in the call.

She wrapped her scarf around her neck and shook her head remembering the wonder on Tyler's face when they took the shortcut off the main highway, hoping to slash some time off their day. The road took them through a beautiful forest, with trees lining both sides of the road as far as they could see. It had been a fun diversion, but now she feared it had been a horrible idea.

It was mid-afternoon, but the dark grey sky made it seem later. The November days were getting shorter. She tucked the heavy blanket closer around her son's neck. She looked in the rearview mirror but could see only the stack of belongings that filled the space in her small SUV and part of the wheels from their bikes strapped to the back.

She shook her leg as she kept her eye on the side mirror watching for the tow truck. She waited less than an hour when she was rewarded with the sight of a gigantic red truck behind her, its orange lights flashing a greeting.

She hopped out of the car and moved toward the driver's window of the tall truck, taking in the festive wreath strapped to its grill. The driver turned and gave her a wave. Abby's eyes widened when she realized the driver was a woman. Abby noticed the reindeer antlers protruding from both sides of the truck windows.

The driver opened her door and hopped down to the ground. "Sorry for the wait. You're a ways from town. I'm Debbie, by the way."

"No problem. I appreciate you coming. My name is Hope and this is my son, Jake. We need to get to a mechanic."

"Sure thing. I'll have us on the road in a few minutes. Go ahead and get your things and you and your son can ride with me in the cab."

Abby hurried back to the car and retrieved her purse and jostled Tyler awake. "Hey, buddy, come on. The car broke down, so we have to get towed to town."

His eyes fluttered as he took in the announcement and looked outside. He gave her a tiny nod and picked up his backpack from the floor. She distracted her son by pointing out the decorations on the truck. By the time Abby got Tyler situated in the cab and buckled in, Debbie already had the car loaded and was at the door.

Debbie jumped into her seat and made a note on her pad of tickets. "Okay, we're off. I'm assuming you don't have a preference on a garage?"

Abby shook her head. "No clue. Can you recommend

someone that does good work and won't take advantage of me?"

"I know just the place. There are only a few shops in town, but Chet's is the best. He and his guys are great and will treat you right."

Abby and Tyler huddled together listening to the jabber of the dispatcher on the radio as they rumbled down the road. After passing by miles of trees and a few fields, they began to see a few houses. As they continued, the number of buildings increased, and they passed a sign welcoming them to Silver Falls.

Debbie took one of the first turns off the main highway and drove a block to Chet's Auto Repair. "I'll let you out here at the office and drop the car around the front," Debbie motioned to the glass door on the side of the metal building. "Do you want to pay with a credit card?"

"Uh, no. I have cash." Abby dug into her purse and rifled in her wallet. She handed Debbie the bills and took a copy of her receipt. "Thanks for the ride," she said, as she helped Tyler down from the truck."

"Best of luck to you, Hope."

Abby nodded and gave a small wave. She hadn't been Abby for two months. Hope was the name she used nowadays. It had belonged to her great-great-grandmother, and Abby was in a place where she could use all the hope she could muster. She trusted it wouldn't prove to be an ironic choice.

2

Practice helped her new name roll off her tongue. It hadn't been easy at first. She told Tyler they were playing a long game of pretend on their great adventure and needed new names. She chose Hope and Tyler wanted to use Jake. The mother and son had been driving across the country since they left Ohio in September.

She took her son's hand and led him through the door. The office was warm, and a hint of something sweet mingled with the odor of grease and oil that had seeped into the walls over time. A television mounted in the corner of the room displayed a show she remembered from her childhood. Dozens of trophies and model cars lined the shelves along the walls. Posters of race car drivers and hot rods covered the remaining space.

A smiling woman peered over the top of the high counter she sat behind and said, "How can I help you?"

Before she could say anything, a man in coveralls burst forth from the door between the office and shop. The clack of air tools and the whine of machinery filled the air. The balding man with "Chet" embroidered on a placket on his chest extended his hand.

"You must be Miss Hope," he glanced at his clipboard, "Quinn?" He smiled at her and said, "I'm Chet. Debbie tells me your car left you stranded outside of town."

She nodded. "That's right. Nice to meet you." She let go of his hand taking note of how clean it was. All the mechanics she had ever met had grimy hands.

"And who is this young man?" Chet said, as he moved through the low swinging door that separated the office staff from the customers. "This is my son, Jake," said Hope.

Chet extended his hand again and then bent down and offered Jake some coloring books and crayons and a toy car. "Amy will get you two some hot chocolate, and you can hang out here while we take a look at the car. If you're hungry, the diner is just a block up the main road."

Hope guided Jake to the restroom to wash his hands while Amy produced two cups of cocoa with tiny marshmallows. The two settled into the chairs along one wall of the customer waiting area. Jake took in an episode of *Mister Ed* while he colored pages in one of the coloring books Chet had suggested.

Hope stared at the clock on the wall as it inched toward five o'clock. A few minutes later, Chet reappeared. "Miss Hope, I've got some bad news. The engine was almost out of oil, and once we added more, it started right up. We started to take it for a test drive to check things and the transmission wouldn't go into gear. We checked it out, and I'm afraid you're going to need a new one."

Hope's face paled. "Oh, no. How much will that be?"

Chet explained she had a couple of choices. He said he would make some calls and get some prices on a rebuilt one and also check on one with a warranty. The warranty option would be more expensive, but if she were planning to travel, it would give her some peace of mind. Hope nodded, willing the burning tears she felt in her eyes not to fall.

Chet gestured to the clock on the wall. "Problem is, it's quitting time. I won't know anything until Monday, at the earliest."

Amy took in Hope's mindless nodding and watched as she rested her hand on her son's head. "I'll make some calls to the motels and see what's available unless you have a place to stay?"

Hope turned her attention to the woman behind the counter. "That would be great. I don't know anyone here. We're just passing through." She added, "It needs to be inexpensive." She lowered her voice to a whisper, "We've been doing quite a bit of camping."

Amy nodded her understanding as Chet turned and raised his eyebrows at his office manager. Amy used the eraser end of a pencil and punched in a number. Hope sighed and helped Jake color farm animals in the coloring book.

Hope listened to Amy inquire about rooms and prices. She waited for her to finish the call and then approached the counter. "I'm going to need to get in the car and get our things."

Chet came through the shop door again. "One of my guys, Matt, called his aunt. She's got a good friend with a bed and breakfast and said to bring you on over. Come on through and get what you need out of the car and I'll drive you over."

Jake stayed in the office with Amy and ran his toy car along the edge of the table while Hope followed Chet to the shop bay and retrieved a suitcase and some other items. She also asked him to put their bicycles in the back of his truck. He helped her load the items and drove around the building.

Hope helped Jake climb into Chet's vintage truck, taking in the spotless interior. She made sure their shoes were clean, and her eyes widened when she saw the modern seatbelts in the old truck. She commented on them, and as Chet drove, he explained his love of the truck and how he had restored it but updated much of the interior to make it more comfortable and convenient.

Chet pulled into a driveway flanked by brick pillars adorned with Christmas wreaths and lights. The driveway led to an inviting two-story Craftsman style home. Hope noticed the lights hung on the posts of the large porch, a ladder, and bins of decorations stacked near the stairs leading up to the entrance. The sign announcing Silver Lake Guest House was adorned with fresh garland and red bows.

Jake's eyes were wide as he stared at the huge house. It looked like something on a Christmas card. Hope glanced at Chet and said, "I'm not sure we can afford this."

"You're in luck. Dottie, needs a little help and had a cancellation. The room is yours free of charge." He parked the truck and opened the door.

Hope swallowed the lump in her throat and fought back tears of happiness. She let out a sigh of relief and unbuckled Jake, handing him his backpack and moving to the back of the truck to help Chet. He secured their bicycles in the rack on the side of the house and helped Hope carry their belongings.

Dottie opened the front door as they stepped onto the porch. She was a tiny woman, but what she lacked in stature, she made up for in exuberance. She reached an arm around Chet's shoulder. "You're just in time for dinner, Chet." She smiled at Hope and said, "I'm so pleased you're here, Hope." She gazed down at the boy and said, "You too, Jake. I could use some help getting ready for the holidays and understand you two need a room for a few days. I've got you set up downstairs in the Blue Room." She gestured them inside and pointed the way.

Dottie led the group to a bedroom suite in the back of the

house, overlooking the landscaped grounds. "This room is lovely, but being on the ground level, it's sometimes the last one chosen because the others have a view of the lake."

"You have a lake?" asked Jake, his eyes wide in disbelief.

"Well, it's not my lake, but you can visit it." She gave the boy a conspiratorial wink. "It's too cold this time of year to do much, but it's perfect in the summer." She took Jake's hand in hers. "How about we let your mom get settled, and you can help me clean up the snacks from the living room? Dinner will be ready soon. I've also got a special friend I want you to meet."

Chet followed Dottie and Jake while Hope went about organizing their clothes and other belongings. It had been weeks since she had slept in a real bed and it had been in a cheap motel along a noisy freeway. She opened the suitcase and placed their clothes inside the antique dresser and stacked Jake's books by the bedside.

She sat on the edge of the bed, covered with a blue duvet that matched the color of the walls. The stack of pillows tempted her. She leaned back against them and detected a hint of lavender. She pulled the soft throw over her legs. The muted blues, grays, and whites decorating the space were peaceful and relaxing. The only light in the room came from a small lamp on the bedside, and as Hope thought about the car and how she would pay to get it fixed, her eyes fluttered shut.

Hope felt a tap on her shoulder and woke with a start two hours later. Jake's face was inches from her own. "Mommy, we saved you some dinner. Dottie said we have to wait for you to have dessert. She's got a dog named Scout." Jake's eyes twinkled with delight as he talked about his new friend.

Hope smiled and hugged Jake. "I'm sorry I fell asleep. I can't believe it's so late. I'll be right there." She hurried to the bathroom and ran a brush through her hair. She found Jake in the large living room on a sofa next to Dottie near the roaring fire. A beautiful golden retriever rested at their feet. Chet was in a leather chair listening to Dottie tell Jake about summers at the lake.

"I'm so embarrassed. I can't believe I slept so long."

"Not to worry, dear. You've had a stressful day." Dottie stood and motioned Hope to follow her. "I've got your plate warming in the oven."

Hope stepped into the huge kitchen lined with vintage white cabinets, a central island, double wall ovens, and a giant restaurant style cooktop. The walnut floors and the dark granite countertops provided a warm contrast to the shades of white found in the paint colors and the subway tiles behind the cooking area.

Dottie used a towel to snatch the plate from the oven and placed it atop a placemat on the large wooden table in the niche off the kitchen. She poured a glass of water and added a lemon slice. "I'll work on our dessert while you eat," she motioned Hope to a chair.

Hope marveled at the plate heaped with roast and mashed potatoes, smothered in rich gravy, accompanied by bright vegetables. The hearty aroma reminded her stomach she hadn't eaten much all day. Dottie returned to the table with a small basket of hot biscuits. "If you need something, give a shout."

Hope dug into the delicious meal. She hadn't tasted a home cooked meal since leaving her own home and relished the flavors. As she ate, she watched Dottie slice something in a baking pan and add it to bowls. Dottie moved to the large freezer and plucked a container of ice cream from the shelf.

She added a healthy scoop to each bowl and placed them on a tray.

Hope hadn't realized how hungry she was. She ate every morsel from her plate as she watched her hostess prepare dessert. Dottie added napkins and spoons to the tray as Hope approached the sink with her dishes.

"Berry cobbler with ice cream. Come out by the fireplace and join us." She gave Hope a wink. "You can bring the coffee pot. Chet probably needs a refill." She pointed her head toward the large counter set up against one wall of the kitchen. It housed an industrial looking coffee machine, a large pot of hot water, hot chocolate mix, teas, and a selection of condiments. A commercial toaster rested next to a covered glass tray of breads and pastries.

Hope took the pot of coffee and made her way to the large living area. Jake was digging into his bowl and listening to Chet's stories of growing up in Silver Falls. Scout stood at attention, watching Jake's progress, sniffing out any crumbs. Hope refilled Chet's coffee and poured herself half a cup before returning it to the beverage counter.

She hunkered down on a sofa, eager to let the warmth of the fire soak into her muscles. Jake finished his bowl and she watched him sink deeper into the cushions, his eyes heavy. She spooned the last bite of her cobbler into her mouth and said, "This was so good, Dottie. I can't begin to thank you for such a wonderful meal."

"I'm glad you enjoyed it, dear. Tomorrow I'll have you help me do a few things around here. I've got one room leaving, so we'll need to clean it and change the linens. The other three rooms are here all weekend. We'll need to freshen them after breakfast."

Hope stood and extended a hand to Chet. "I'm grateful for your help today. I'll talk to you Monday when you know more about the costs." She collected their empty dishes on the tray and turned to her son. "I'm going to get Jake to bed."

"See you in the morning. I start in the kitchen at six," said Dottie, resting her hand atop Scout's head.

Chet said his goodbyes and made for the door, where he found a couple on the porch just returning from their evening meal. The man and woman gave a wave and murmured a greeting before ascending the stairs.

As Hope helped Jake from the couch, half carrying him, Scout gave him a lick on the cheek. "Sweet girl," said Hope. "I love her name."

Dottie smiled. "*To Kill a Mockingbird* is a favorite book of mine." She petted the dog and added, "She's my constant companion and a great partner."

Hope looked back from the hallway and saw Dottie gazing at a photo on the side table. She heard her whisper to Scout, "I know girl, I miss him too."

3

Hope's phone vibrated and a soft buzz rang out next to her ear early the next morning. She tiptoed through the bedroom, leaving Jake to sleep while she got ready for the day.

She made her way to the kitchen and found Dottie arranging fresh pastries on trays. "Wow, what time did you get up to bake these?"

Dottie smiled, "Good morning. I cheat on my pastries. My son owns a bakery, and I get a delivery from him each morning. Saves me lots of time and they're as good as my own." She winked and nodded toward the beverage counter. "Help yourself to something, and then we'll get to cooking breakfast."

The twosome found a rhythm and worked together to whip up pancakes and an egg and sausage bake. Guests began filtering into the large breakfast niche off the kitchen, helping themselves to coffee. Dottie made sure she introduced Hope to each of them, presenting her as a friend who would be helping out for a few days.

As soon as she was done squeezing the oranges for juice,

Hope dashed back to the bedroom to check on Jake. He was lounging in bed reading one of his books and Scout had positioned herself next to him on the bed. Hope smiled as her son read to the dog. "Breakfast is ready. How about you get dressed and come join us?"

He put the book down and gathered his clothes and went into the bathroom. Scout followed at his heels. Hope started to call the dog and then shook her head. "Do you need some help?"

"No, I'm okay." Jake ushered the dog into the bathroom and shut the door.

Hope shrugged and chuckled as she made the bed and straightened the room while she listened for Jake. He emerged in clean clothes with his hair combed and Scout at his side. Hope checked him over and said, "Bath tonight, buddy."

He nodded with enthusiasm. "I saw that cool bathtub in there."

"You can try it out tonight. Let's go have breakfast and then you can finish reading to Scout." She took his hand and led him to the kitchen.

The guests had gathered around the oversized wooden table and were busy eating and chatting. The couples, all middle-aged or older, welcomed Jake and doted upon him as they finished their breakfasts.

Scout rested on her bed near the kitchen door that led outside to a beautiful sitting area. Dottie helped the couple checking out and processed their credit card, while the others lingered over coffee.

As soon as Jake gobbled down the remaining bites of his pancakes, he hurried to the living room, and Scout trotted after him. Hope gathered dirty dishes and had cleared the table when Dottie returned.

"They were in the Plum Room upstairs. We'll get these

dishes done up, and then I'll show you what I need done to get their room cleaned and ready for the next guests. I'm booked solid this weekend, except for your room."

Hope loaded the dishwasher while Dottie tidied the counters and gathered the remaining cups once the guests left the table to start their day. Hope checked on Jake who was sprawled in front of the fire, leaning against Scout with his book. She followed Dottie upstairs.

The innkeeper showed her a storage closet where she kept cleaning supplies and linens for all the rooms. They changed the bed and gathered sheets and towels before disinfecting the bathroom, wiping down all the surfaces in the bedroom, and doing the floors. Dottie showed Hope how to restock the toiletries and other amenities in the room and pronounced it done. "That's a lot easier with help," she said with a smile.

"Let's check the towels in the other rooms while we're here." She knocked on each door and found the rooms empty. Dottie gathered towels guests had left to be exchanged and nodded her head with satisfaction when she found all the beds had been made. The pair made quick work of disinfecting the bathrooms and replacing towels.

"We don't do full housekeeping unless guests are here more than three days. Most of our guests are like these folks, neat and tidy, so it doesn't take much." She handed Hope the remaining towels and led her to a laundry room at the end of the hallway. It served as a powder room and had been remodeled to house the laundry equipment. She went through the motions of how to work the machines and started a load. She charged Hope with taking care of the laundry for the day.

"Okay," said Dottie, "now let's get to work on some Christmas decorations. We can get Jake to help us."

She led the way downstairs and down the hall to a large

storage room. Hope noticed the library niche built in the area beneath the stairs. The underside of the stairway was fashioned as bookcases. "What a lovely spot for reading," she said.

Dottie smiled and said, "I saw this in a magazine and showed my husband. Next thing I knew he was building it. It's a cozy reading spot. Feel free to try it out."

They retrieved plastic totes from storage and stacked them along the wall. Scout's nails tapped across the wooden floors as she hurried to the front door. A tall man opened the door and hollered out, "Mom, it's just me."

A flash of copper and ebony fur dashed through the open door. Two dogs trotted to the living room sniffing out Scout. Dottie yelled, "I'm in here," as she shut the door to the storage room. "Getting Christmas decorations out and organized."

The man came around the corner, and Dottie said, "Grant, I'd like you to meet Hope. She's helping me out for a few days." She turned her head to Hope. "Grant is my youngest son who owns the bakery." The dark-haired man, with a five o'clock shadow, flashed Hope a grin and extended his hand.

His blue eyes sparkled with warmth. Hope took his hand and said, "Nice to meet you."

"I thought I'd help get some of those outside lights strung," said Grant. "I'll take the three hooligans outside, and they can romp around while I work."

Dottie led the pair to the living room where Jake was giggling in the midst of the three playful dogs. "I see you've met Ginger and Luna," said Dottie, smiling at her granddogs surrounding the young boy. Ginger was redder than Scout, but a typical lovable golden retriever. Luna had the happy smile of a Labrador and her sleek black fur looked like it had been polished.

"Would you like to help me wrangle these three trouble-makers outside," asked Grant.

Jake looked at his mom, and she gave him a nod of approval. "You behave for Grant. He's Dottie's son."

Jake eyes traveled over Grant. "Wow, you're big for a son."

Grant chuckled and offered Jake a hand. He soon had the dogs outside and gave Jake the task of keeping them busy with a game of fetch while he got to work on the ladder.

Hope kept busy with the laundry and helped Dottie scour the kitchen and put together some appetizers for the afternoon. After she finished in the kitchen, she poked her head outside to check on Jake. She found him in the yard with a total of five dogs. She also saw another set of legs on a ladder at the other end of the house.

"Are you doing okay, Jake?" she yelled from the porch.

He turned and gave her several exaggerated nods of his head amid giggles. The furry newcomers noticed her and dashed to the porch. Before she knew it, two golden retrievers were slammed against her legs begging to be petted.

Jake clomped up the stairs. "Mom, this is Fletch and Dickens," he said, patting their heads.

"Where did they come from?" she asked, giving each of them nuzzles.

Jake pointed at the end of the house where the extra set of legs on the ladder still stood. "Drew brought them."

"Are you warm enough?" she asked, noticing Jake's red cheeks.

He nodded and scurried down the steps, the dogs chasing him back to the other three. "Bye," he screeched as the dogs ran by him.

Hope went back inside and hurried upstairs to fold the clean laundry. When she returned, she found Dottie sitting by the fire with a pot of tea beside her. "Let's have a nice cup before everyone gets back home, shall we?"

Hope accepted the cup and a warm cookie. "We need to sample our work before the guests eat them. Wouldn't want to serve something inedible." Dottie gave her a sly wink and took another cookie from the plate.

"These are delicious," said Hope. She finished the frosted pumpkin cookie and sipped her tea.

"I like to have some nibbles available for the guests in the afternoon." She held her cup of tea and gazed out the window. "I see Jake met my other granddogs. They belong to my oldest son, Drew."

Hope nodded. "Jake is having the time of his life playing with all of them."

"We're definitely dog people." Dottie glanced at the clock. "I promised the boys dinner tonight for helping me. I guess I better get moving."

"I've got everything done upstairs. I can help." Hope gathered the tray of tea goodies and followed Dottie to the kitchen.

Dottie assigned Hope a few jobs, and they had dinner in the oven in under an hour. They sat at the large table the guests had used for breakfast. Dottie scribbled on a notepad. "I've got to get organized for Thanksgiving. I think I have it all and then remember something else."

The clomp of feet and the sound of dozens of toenails on the wooden floors announced the arrival of the men, a boy, and five dogs. The men guided Jake and the dogs to the mudroom off the back entrance. She heard the water running as hands were washed. The dogs piled onto soft beds lining the wall, waiting for treats to be distributed. Grant came around the corner and filled a cup from the large coffee pot and made his way to the table. "It's getting cold," he said, warming his hands around the cup.

Jake arrived, followed by Drew, who was holding two cups. He placed a hot chocolate on the table and Jake scrambled into the chair in front of it. Drew slid in next to his brother.

"Oh, I haven't introduced you," Dottie said. "Hope, this is my eldest, Drew. Hope is Jake's mom."

The tall man with blondish hair threaded with gray, nodded in Hope's direction. She moved to shake his hand, but he didn't return the gesture. "Nice to meet you," she said.

"Did you boys get all the decorations done?" asked Dottie.

They nodded in unison. "I think you're ready for the holidays," said Grant.

"I've still got the inside to get done. Not to mention Thanksgiving. Hope's going to get a workout." Dottie gave her a wink over the rim of her cup.

Hope glanced at her son. "We're happy to help decorate or do anything else you need done."

Drew put his hand atop his mother's. "Mom goes all out for the holidays."

Grant smiled and added, "She even transformed Dad into her elf."

A tear slid down Dottie's cheek. "It's our first year without him. Curt, my husband."

Drew's hand tightened and gripped his mother's. "We lost Dad in January. It's been hard on all of us, but especially Mom. This place takes a lot of work."

"You boys have been such a help. I know how hard it is for you to juggle your businesses and help me." She turned to Hope. "You know Grant is the baker. Drew is the local veterinarian."

A cell phone rang out and Drew reached to his belt. "Dr. Fisher," he said, standing and moving away from the table.

Moments later he returned and said, "I've got an emergency. A dog got trampled by a horse. I'll be back as soon as I can." He leaned in and gave his mom a peck on the cheek.

"Leave the dogs here. Jake can entertain them." She saw the boy's eyes dance with excitement as he nodded in agreement." He scrambled from the table, intent on watching his charges.

Jake wasn't gone long and approached the table with his head hanging. "They're all asleep."

"Once we start rustling around in the kitchen, I guarantee they'll be awake." Dottie looked at the clock. "We'll give Drew some time to get back before we start." She reached for her notepad. "I'm going to finish my list for Thanksgiving."

"How about we go watch something on television, Jake?" asked Grant. He led the boy through the living room and into the private wing of the house to a large family room.

While Dottie perused her lists, Hope cut up potatoes and put them in a pot, checked the applesauce they had started earlier, and at Dottie's direction, stirred together ingredients to make a glaze for the baking ham.

Hope and Dottie set the table. "Well, we best start things. I'll keep a plate warm for Drew," said Dottie with a sigh. "He's the only vet in town, and it seems like he never gets a weekend off."

They finished the dinner prep with four attentive dogs watching their every move, waiting for something edible to drop to the floor. Dottie asked Hope to retrieve the boys from the family room.

Hope made her way down the hall and noticed the family photos on the wall leading into the more private part of the house. She found Grant and Jake dozing on a sofa with the television turned to a fishing show. Scout had escaped from the mudroom and was sprawled next to Jake.

She crept toward the sleeping trio. Scout's ears perked

when Hope got close. She nudged Jake awake and whispered, "Time for dinner, sweetie."

Scout jumped from the couch, and the commotion woke Grant. He opened his eyes and said, "Must be time to eat." He scooted Jake off the couch and said, "That dog speaks better English than most people. She knows what dinner means."

"Your mom sent me to get you guys to the table." She took Jake's hand and led him from the room. Her eyes focused on a photo of a younger Drew with a beautiful woman and a smiling young boy. "Oh, that must be Drew's family?"

Grant sighed. "It was. His wife and son died in a car accident years ago."

She brought her hand to her mouth to cover her gasp. "Oh, I'm so sorry." She urged Jake to follow Scout to the kitchen.

Grant stopped in front of the photos and in a low voice said, "Danny was only seven. A big rig ran a light and t-boned them. Laura and Danny died at the scene. It was horrible."

Hope sucked in a breath. "That's awful. Poor Drew. I'm sure his life has never been the same."

Grant nodded. "I don't think he's ever recovered. With dad's death, it brought it all back to the surface for all of us. It hasn't been easy." He continued down the hall while Hope lingered and looked at the smiling faces of Drew, Laura, and little Danny.

She shuddered and hurried to catch up to Grant. She helped Dottie get platters and serving bowls filled and on the table. As soon as they picked up their forks, they heard the dogs scramble to the front door to greet Drew.

They led him into the kitchen. "Sorry, I hope you didn't wait on me."

Dottie waved him to the chair next to her. "You're just in time. We just sat down."

They chatted as they devoured the hearty meal. Hope insisted Dottie relax while she took care of the dishes. Mother and sons, along with all the dogs, retired to the living area and sat in front of the fire. Jake helped Hope clear the table and then joined the others.

By the time Hope finished the kitchen chores, her son was fast asleep atop Scout, surrounded by the other dozing dogs. "Looks like they're all worn out," said Hope.

"They're not the only ones." Drew stood and gave his mom a quick kiss. "I need to get back to the office and check on the dog."

"I should get going, too. I've got some work to get to," said Grant. He kneeled in front of his mother and wrapped her in a hug. "See you tomorrow, Mom."

After the boys and their dogs left, the house was much quieter. Hope wished Dottie a pleasant night and bundled Jake into her arms. She got him in bed and crawled in beside him. She made sure her phone alarm was set. As she drifted to sleep, a single tear slid from her eye and plopped onto the pillow.

4

Hope and Dottie spent the morning occupied with breakfast duties and tidying the rooms. After some homemade soup and some of Grant's delicious fresh bread for lunch, Dottie gave Hope directions to the lake and suggested she take Jake and Scout for an adventure.

"I'm going to make my cranberry sauce and prep a few things for Thursday. You go have some fun and enjoy our beautiful lake."

Hope decided to ride bikes since Dotty told her there was a nice road all the way to the lake. They took off with Scout jogging beside them. Within a few minutes, they saw the signs for Silver Lake. They followed the arrows and came to the small RV park Dottie had described. The sign announced it was closed for the winter and reservation inquiries could be made by contacting Silver Lake Guest House.

They continued down the road and came to a clearing in the woods, and Jake screeched with excitement. "Look, Mommy, it's the lake!"

She smiled and grabbed his bike as he and Scout took off for the shoreline. "Stay out of the water, Jake," she yelled.

She leaned their bikes against a tree and hurried after the pair. Scout was chasing Jake, who was laughing and screaming. She picked up a few rocks and began skipping them across the water. Jake stopped running and watched his mother.

"Can I try?" he asked.

She handed him several rocks and then showed him the technique she used to hold the rock and snap it across the water. They used all the rocks she had gathered without Jake achieving success. She led him along the edge of the water and showed him how to pick out the larger flat rocks she liked to use.

As they collected, Jake asked, "Who taught you to skip rocks, Mommy?"

"My daddy. Grandpa Lloyd."

"Oh, yeah, I was a baby when he died, right?"

She nodded and reminded him her parents had both passed away soon after his birth. She pushed the memories away and focused her attention on the rocks.

With their jacket pockets full, they set about launching more stones. They were down to the last rock when Jake finally got it to skip three times. He jumped in the air and shouted, causing Scout to abandon her search of the trees and come running.

"I did it. I did it. That was so fun," he said, cheeks reddened from the cold. "Let's do more."

"We need to get going. We can come back another day."

Jake stuck out his lip but snapped it back in place with one look from Hope. Scout trotted ahead of them as they rode back to the guest house. They came in the back door and took off their shoes and stowed their jackets on the hooks. Scout slurped water from her bowl and Hope suggested hot chocolate.

When Scout finished her drink, she bolted from the

mudroom and hurried through the house. Curious, Hope followed. She gasped when she saw Dottie sprawled on the stairs. Christmas ornaments and decorations littered the steps. Soft moans came from the woman as Hope reached her.

She crouched down to her. "Dottie, what happened?"

Tears stained her cheeks, and her eyes squinted with pain. "I was carrying a box and tripped."

"I'll call an ambulance." Hope stood. "I'll be right back."

Dottie waved her hand. "No, no. Just call Drew. He'll know what to do." My cell phone is in the kitchen.

Hope hurried to the kitchen and scanned the counters. She snatched the phone and scrolled through the contacts until she found him. He answered on the second ring.

"Hey, Mom. I was just coming over."

"Drew, it's Hope. Jake and I just got in from the lake and found your mom. She fell on the stairs and wanted me to call you instead of an ambulance."

"I'll be right there." He disconnected before Hope could say more.

She told Jake to stay in the kitchen and grabbed pillows from the living room before hurrying back to Dottie. She put a pillow under her head and said, "Drew is on his way."

Scout had stayed at Dottie's side, licking her hand, then her cheek, and whimpering. Hope patted the dog's head. "It's okay, girl. Help is on the way." The dog's gentle eyes gazed at Dottie, and she nestled closer to her owner.

Less than a minute later, Hope heard the front door bang open and fast-moving footsteps. Drew rushed up the stairs. Hope moved out of the way to give him room and went to check on Jake. She found him wide-eyed and pale.

"What happened?" he whispered.

She explained about Dottie's accident while she fixed him

a hot chocolate. "You stay here for a few minutes while I see if Drew needs help."

Drew was still examining Dottie. He raised his eyes to meet Hope's. "Good news is there's no neck or back issues. I think she probably fractured her leg or ankle. Can't tell, but we need to get her to the hospital."

Hope helped him, and together they carried Dottie from the stairs to a chair near the front door. Drew dialed his phone while Hope retrieved Dottie's coat. He disconnected and said, "Okay, Mom. I called the ER, and they know we're on our way. They're calling Doc Stevens now."

He opened the front door and moved his SUV closer to the walkway. His two dogs hurried behind him and into the house. In a stern voice, he told them to sit and made Scout join them in front of the fireplace. "Okay," he said, coming back to the front door. "This is the shortest route, albeit it has stairs. Are you up to helping me get her down them?" He looked at Hope with raised brows.

"Yeah, I can do it." She gave him a nod and rushed to get her jacket. They made a makeshift chair with their arms linked and supported Dottie all the way down the stairs.

Once she was in the seat, Drew shut the door and hurried around to the driver's side. "I've got to leave the dogs here. I'll be back as soon as I can. I'll call Grant on my way."

Before she could respond, he jumped into the SUV. Hope made her way to the kitchen, found Jake, and hung up her coat. "Let's sit by the fire with the dogs. Drew needs us to watch them."

Jake's somber face lit up with excitement at her mention of his new furry friends. She got him settled and went about collecting the decorations still scattered on the stairs. She returned them to the box and put it in the storage room.

It was past dinner. She knew there was soup from lunch and leftovers from last night. She started building a platter of ham sandwiches and heated up the soup. She wanted to wait for everyone to get home but knew Jake needed to eat.

She sat with him while he ate his dinner. She convinced him to take a bath only when she agreed all three dogs could keep him company. Once she got him in, he lingered and played until the water went cold.

He put on his jammies, and she tucked him into bed. The three dogs joined him with Scout snuggled the closest. She plucked a book from his stack and left him reading to his audience.

She added a log to the fire and wandered into the kitchen. Her stomach grumbled, so she fixed a small plate and ate. She heard the front door open and scrambled from her chair. It was only a couple returning to their room.

She finished her meal and busied herself tidying the kitchen. She saw a recipe card on the counter for a breakfast casserole. Knowing Dottie would be stressed if things weren't ready for her guests, she went about putting together the casserole.

She was doing the dishes when she heard the front door open and voices. She dried her hands and rushed to the entry. Scout was already at the door when Hope arrived. Grant and Drew were helping Dottie, who was now outfitted with a clumsy boot on one leg. Grant ushered his two dogs into the living room and let them give Dottie's leg a good sniff.

They settled Dottie in her favorite chair near the fireplace with Scout's head on her thigh. Grant retrieved her crutches and placed them next to her. "How are you, Dottie?" asked Hope.

She shook her head in disgust. "I can't believe I did this." Tears filled her eyes. "I feel so stupid."

Hope bent down and held her hand. "How about some dinner?"

Grant said, "That would be great. I'm starving. I'm sure you're hungry, Mom." He tapped Hope on the shoulder. "I'll help you get it together."

Hope retrieved the sandwich tray and popped the soup in the microwave. "What did they say about your mom's injury?"

Grant readied a tray with dishes and utensils. "She fractured a bone in her lower leg. She needs to keep it elevated and wear the boot for about eight weeks."

"Oh, poor Dottie." Hope stirred the soup and hit the button to resume cooking.

"She hasn't quite come to terms with the limitations it's going to put on her. The ability to be an innkeeper. Thanksgiving. It's going to be overwhelming." The dogs were interested in the kitchen activities, prompting Grant to inquire about their dinner.

Hope confirmed she hadn't known when or what to feed them. Grant took her in the mudroom and showed her the supplies and how to measure their food. As soon as the dogs heard the sound of kibble being dispensed, they thundered to their bowls. Scout was the only absent one.

Grant fixed Scout's bowl and placed it on the counter next to the tray.

"I'm happy to help. I can take care of the rooms. I found a recipe on the counter and made it for breakfast tomorrow. I figured she'd be too tired to deal with it tonight."

He smiled. "That's terrific. Thanks for doing that. Drew and I talked a bit at the hospital. Neither of us has the time to run this place and our own businesses."

"I'm going to need to do something while my car is getting fixed. If Dottie tells me what to do, I'm sure I can learn."

She added a bowl of soup to the tray, and Grant lifted it

from the counter. "Maybe you can sit with Mom while she eats. That will give us some time to talk about options."

"Of course." She followed with Scout's bowl and cleared off the table next to Dottie's chair to make room for the tray.

"Here you go, Mom. Hope fixed up a nice dinner from our leftovers." Grant motioned his head back toward the kitchen. "Drew, ours is waiting in the kitchen."

The two boys left, and Hope positioned the tray across Dottie's lap and chatted with her while she nibbled at her food. "I suppose you and Jake ate already?" asked Dottie. She glanced at Scout, who ate from her bowl, still watching her master.

"We did. Jake was hungry and tired. He had a bath and read to the dogs."

Dottie smiled. "That's so sweet. They love having a child around the house."

They chatted while Dottie finished her meal. Hope let her know the ornaments were safe in the storage closet and the breakfast casserole was in the fridge.

"Oh, dear. Thank you for doing that. It completely slipped my mind." Tears dotted her cheeks. "I'm going to have to cancel some reservations. There's no way I can keep up with this."

Hope helped her and removed the tray from her lap. "How about a cup of tea?"

Dottie agreed, and Hope withdrew to the kitchen. She found Grant and Drew at the island with remnants of their dinners in front of them. She slid the tray onto the counter and retrieved cups for tea.

In a low voice, Drew said, "Grant tells me you're willing to stay and help Mom here with the guests."

"Yes, I've got a mess of my own to sort out, so I'm more than happy to help Dottie. She's been wonderful to me." She added napkins to the tea tray she'd prepared. "She's worried she's going to have to cancel reservations."

The boys nodded and Grant said, "Let's talk to Mom and see what she says." He grabbed the tray and said, "Let me carry that."

The four other dogs followed behind them and flopped down in front of the fireplace. Scout stayed next to Dottie.

Over tea they talked about the guest house and the idea of Hope helping Dottie run it for a few weeks. "Are you sure about this, dear?" asked Dottie.

Hope smiled and nodded. "I'm sure."

"We'll need you to fill out an employment application and check your references. Are you sure your schedule is that flexible?" asked Drew.

"Nonsense, Drew. She's not applying for a job. She's trying to help," said Dottie.

Hope turned to face Drew. "I don't have a timetable to keep. Jake and I are on an adventure. I homeschool him, and we're trying to visit all the states this year as part of his learning. No tight schedules to keep. With my vehicle situation, I'm stranded until it's resolved."

"Let's try it for a week and see how it goes. If it's too much for you or Mom, we'll figure out a different solution," suggested Grant.

Drew pursed his lips but said nothing. He stood and showed Hope Dottie's medication and a schedule he penned on a notepad. "Make sure you log everything on the schedule." He turned to Dottie. "Let's get you situated in your room, Mom. I'll stop by on my way to work in the morning and check on you."

Hope offered to add her cell phone number to Dottie's cell. "That way if you need help during the night, just call me, and I'll be right there."

Hope wished them good night and left them to get their

mother situated. When they heard her door close, Drew said, "Are you sure this is a good idea, Mom? We don't know anything about her? She could be a con artist."

Grant rolled his eyes. "I really don't think she's a scammer. She's here by chance because of her car. She's pitched in without being asked." His tone betrayed his annoyance with his brother.

Dottie put down her cup. "Drew, I know you don't always trust easily, but I have a good feeling about Hope. She's a sweet woman and Jake is a polite and smart little boy. She needs a bit of help, and I could use a hand. It'll be fine."

Drew shook his head. "Okay, but if anything seems off, you need to speak up, Mom. Grant will be by like usual early in the morning, and I'll stop by on my way to the office and when I get off."

"Just call if you need anything. I can be here in minutes," said Grant.

"It'll work out, boys. I think Hope's here for a reason."

5

Hope was in the kitchen before six. She checked on Dottie, who was still asleep. She urged Scout to follow her and left the bedroom door open so the dog could come and go. She went about getting breakfast ready. Grant came through the back door with a box of fresh pastries as she was getting the coffee brewing.

"How was your night?" he asked.

"Uneventful. I just checked on Dottie, and she was still sleeping. I would imagine those meds are to blame."

He nodded. "Drew said they'd make her drowsy." He offered to feed Scout, and the dog approached her breakfast with enthusiasm. She leaned against Grant, begging for a good nuzzle.

"Drew was going to look into getting a home health nurse to check on Mom. He'll be by before nine." He gave Scout's chin a scratch and waved goodbye. While the casserole finished baking, she dashed to her room and got Jake up and ready. Scout followed and sat on the floor until Jake trailed his mother to the kitchen.

The casserole, pastries, and a bit of fruit provided a

substantial breakfast for the guests. Hope visited with them and explained about Dottie's fall. All of them were checking out today, and Hope knew her day would be harried. Hope surveyed the registration book Dottie kept in the desk and saw all of them had prepaid their stays. That meant she had a few hours to have Dottie teach her how to run her credit card machine.

Jake finished breakfast and took his books into the living room with Scout. The guests were quick to eat and left with their luggage. Drew arrived as the last couple was loading their car.

He gave Hope a stern nod and disappeared down the hall to his mother's wing of the house. Thirty minutes later he returned trailing Dottie as he instructed her on using her crutches.

"Good morning, Dottie. Would you like some breakfast?" asked Hope.

"Coffee sounds wonderful," she said with a small smile.

Hope made plates for Drew and his mother and delivered coffees to the table. Dottie was propped in a chair with her bad leg resting on an adjacent one. As they ate, Drew explained a nurse would be stopping by to check on Dottie and help her with bathing and getting things set up around the house.

"I've got Mom set up in the family room, so she can watch television and not be disturbed by the guests," he added, finishing the last bite from his plate.

"I looked in your book, and there is just one couple checking in today. I'll make that room the priority and get to work on all the other rooms. We'll be full on Wednesday, including the Blue Room."

Dottie bobbed her head. "You and Jake can move into the guest room next to mine. It's not much and it's small, but it will work in a pinch. The Monday after Thanksgiving, we'll be back down to a small number of guests."

Drew finished his breakfast and took his last swig of coffee. "I'll get Mom settled before I leave. You've got our numbers, so just call if you need anything. Grant and I will take turns bringing dinner over each night. Grant volunteered to take tonight."

Minutes after Drew left, Grant came through the door. He bent down next to Dottie's recliner. "I had a few minutes and thought I'd check on you."

Hope brought Dottie a cup of tea and offered to fix something for Grant. "No, I've only got a few minutes. I've been drinking coffee all morning." He moved to sit on the couch. "We discussed your new duties, Hope, and want to pay you for the extra work."

She held up her hands. "It's not necessary. I'm thankful to have a place to stay. Let's just see how it goes, shall we?"

"Now, Hope, you're going to need money to fix your car," said Dottie. "You keep track of your hours, and we'll come to an agreement before you leave. There's a big difference between a little help and running the whole place on your own."

Hope shrugged. "We'll worry about it later. I'm going to get started on the rooms."

"Oh, what about Thanksgiving?" Dottie's voice cracked and her eyes filled.

"Don't worry about it, Mom. We can handle it. You can supervise." He added with a laugh, "It won't be as good, but we'll manage."

Hope checked on Jake and got him started on his schoolwork and then hurried upstairs. As she was stripping the Rose Room, she sensed someone and turned to see Grant leaning in the doorway.

"She's all set. She asked Jake to join her in the family

room. He's doing his work at the desk in there. She promised no television until he was done."

"Sometimes I feel like a hostage negotiator with him. He'll probably try to finagle a way out of his schoolwork. I'll check on them when I get this laundry going."

Grant picked up the mound of sheets on the floor and carried them to the laundry room. She followed with another pile of towels.

He watched as she turned dials and added detergent. "Thank you for doing this. We appreciate all your help."

Hope raised her brows. "I get the feeling Drew isn't too fond of me being here."

"He's just…extra cautious. He'll come around." Grant sighed. "Anyway, we know this probably wasn't what you had in mind."

"I've learned not to have much in mind. It'll be fine. I'll see you tonight."

He gave her a small salute and headed downstairs. She finished the Rose Room and took a break to check on Jake and her patient. She found Dottie napping in her recliner and Jake still working. Scout was resting against the side of Dottie's chair.

She whispered and pointed at Jake's paper, reminding him to check his work. "How about you read a book, and I'll help you go over this when I finish my work? I'm almost done upstairs."

He nodded and retrieved a book and nestled into the fluffy couch. Scout moved from her position and joined him. Hope took a peek at the guest room next to Dottie's. It had two twin beds and had a few trophies and pennants on the shelves. She suspected it had been the childhood room of Drew and Grant.

Hope hurried back upstairs to finish the rooms. It was close to lunch when she had the room ready and another load in the washer. She found Dottie wide awake, chatting with Jake about the book he had read. There was also a new stack of books on the table. With their vintage titles and covers, they were sure to be leftovers from Dottie's sons.

"Are you two ready for some lunch?"

"How about grilled cheese? You'll find everything you need in the fridge and the pantry," suggested Dottie. "We can go over my reservation book after lunch and get organized for the week."

Scout followed Hope to the kitchen and sat at attention while she put together the cheese sandwiches. She rewarded Scout with a tiny nibble of cheese and several bites of the apples she'd cut up to go with their lunch. She added Dottie's medication to the tray and carried it down the hallway.

As they ate, Dottie reviewed her reservations and made plans to call those arriving on Wednesday to confirm. Hope wouldn't have to move out of the Blue Room if one of them cancelled. She showed Hope her menu plans for breakfast and made a shopping list for the coming week.

Hope suggested they use the leftover breakfast casserole tomorrow for the one couple arriving today. That would give her time to work on the recipes for the rest of the week. Dottie reorganized the menus for the coming weeks, filling most days with easy make-ahead dishes to take some of the pressure off Hope.

"Grant can handle the shopping and ordering. He orders most of my staples through the bakery. While I'm out of commission, we won't offer any extras. At times I prepare dinners or picnics and such, but we need to keep it simple."

Hope gathered their plates and dropped them off in the kitchen on her way to take care of the laundry upstairs. When she returned, Jake was reading to Dottie and Scout.

"I told Jake you could show me your lesson plans for him and while you're doing my work, Jake and I can do his schoolwork. That will give me something to do. I'll go crazy just sitting here all day," said Dottie.

Hope retrieved the satchel with Jake's schoolwork and ran through the materials, showing Dottie the workbooks and lessons. "You're very organized. This looks like a great program."

"I did some research and planning when I knew I'd be homeschooling him this year. It's one of the top-rated programs and much easier than trying to figure it all out myself."

"That's wise. Plus, Jake gets to see so much of the country and learn about history and nature up-close and personal. I think it's fabulous," said Dottie, smiling at Jake.

"I've got lots of cookies and brownies in the freezer out in the mudroom. So, pick some of them, and we'll use them for afternoon treats this week. When things calm down, we can work on making more. Drew texted me and said my nurse will arrive tomorrow, so I'll know more about what to expect after her visit."

Hope checked the clock and saw it was nearing check-in time. She darted to the freezer and plucked out containers of cookies and dashed back upstairs to finish folding laundry. She had Dottie show her the credit card and registration process, which turned out to be easy.

As they were finishing, she heard the bells chime for the front door. She smiled at Chet through the glass. "Hello, Chet. Do you have news?" She led him into the entryway.

"I've got some information. It's not the best news, but here it goes." He explained the costs associated with both of Hope's options, and when he gave her the final figure on a transmission with a warranty, she sucked in her breath.

"Wow, I need to think about this and figure out what to do. Can you give me a bit of time?"

"Sure, no hurry. We heard about Dottie's accident and

from what Grant said, it sounds like you're going to help out here for a bit. It will do her good to have you around." A couple appeared at the front door, luggage in hand.

Chet gave Hope a quick smile and touched his fingers to his cap. "You take your time and give me a shout if you have any questions." He scooted out the door and held it open for the new guests.

Hope greeted the couple, who were in town visiting their son for Thanksgiving. After breathing a sigh of relief when the credit card gizmo worked without a hitch, she gave them a quick tour of the public areas, explained about breakfast, and showed them the complimentary beverage bar. She led them to the Rose Room and left them to get settled.

When she checked on Dottie, she found her and Jake engrossed in a television show. Scout was the only one who noticed Hope's appearance. She crept back down the hall and made herself a cup of tea and swiped a cookie from the tray.

She settled into a chair by the fire and read over the menus and recipes Dottie had shown her in preparation for the week. Grant came through the front door with his two dogs before she had finished her tea.

"Dinner is served," he said, toting a large bag. "Hope you like Italian." She followed him into the kitchen. He began removing containers from the bag. "How's Mom?"

"She's doing well. She and Jake spent the day together while I did things around here. I've still got to make the beds up in two rooms, and I'll be all set for Wednesday." She set the table as she chatted.

Drew came through the back door with Fletch and Dickens, who were joined by the other two dogs. All four focused their attention on their empty food bowls on the floor of the mudroom. They gave him their best sad eyes. Scout appeared moments later.

Drew laughed as he went about filling their bowls. "These

guys never miss a meal." He joined Grant and said, "Smells good. I'll go get Mom."

Several minutes later, Jake came into the kitchen trailed by Dottie and Drew. They settled into chairs around the dining table and Hope helped Grant deliver serving dishes filled with pasta and sauces, garlic bread, and a crisp salad.

As they ate, Grant and Drew shared snippets from their days at work. Jake's eyes brightened when Drew described a litter of new puppies he had examined. "Could we get a puppy, Mom?"

Hope raised her brows and said, "Not right now, Jake. Remember, we're on our adventure this year. It wouldn't be fair to a puppy to be on the road all the time."

Dottie chimed in with her agreement. "Yes, and while you're here, you can help with Scout. She loves to walk, and I'll need someone to take over that job for me while my leg heals."

His thoughts of a new puppy were replaced with chatter about Scout and where they could walk and how far they could travel. He rattled off questions faster than anyone could answer. With the patience only bestowed on grand-mothers, Dottie listened and explained the instructions for walking Scout.

Hope cleared the table, and she and Grant stowed the leftovers while Drew helped Dottie field dog questions. "I think there's plenty here. We won't need to worry about getting anything tomorrow," Hope said, putting the salad in a container.

"That's good. Drew can take Wednesday. I'll be tied up with prep work for Thanksgiving.

She finished wiping the counters and said, "I'm going to run upstairs and finish those two rooms while you and your brother are here for your mom." She glanced at Jake still wide-eyed listening to tales from the animal clinic.

It didn't take Hope long to make the beds and double check things. She made sure all the clean laundry was folded, and all the rooms were ready for visitors. She found the group in the living room surrounded by dogs.

They were eating slices of cake and chatting. Grant spotted Hope and motioned her to the spot on the sofa next to him. "I brought home a cake from the bakery. Here's your slice."

She smiled and thanked him, noting the smears of chocolate frosting decorating Jake's lips and cheeks. "Looks like it's yummy." He gave a few exaggerated nods of his head and a chocolatey smile. She took the plate and a seat next to Grant.

Dottie said, "We were just discussing the rest of the week. I got in touch with all the guests, and they're all confirmed, so you and Jake will have to move into the guest room by me until after the weekend. Then we'll do our best to make sure the Blue Room isn't reserved."

Hope nodded her understanding. "Not a problem. We're just happy to have such a lovely place to stay."

"Drew said he's going to come by tomorrow morning and show me how to walk Scout. He's going to bring Fletch and Dickens." Jake was bouncing in his chair with excitement.

Despite the sugar-laden cake, Jake's eyes drooped with exhaustion. Hope took him by the hand and wished them all a good night.

"Oh, by the way," Grant said, "I left you a box of fresh blueberry scones for tomorrow's breakfast. I'll be late because our food delivery is arriving. I'll stop by later in the day with Mom's groceries."

"Sounds great. See you all tomorrow," said Hope, guiding Jake to their room.

She stuffed him into his pajamas, and he was asleep before she pulled the covers over him. The amount of money she needed for the car repair made her head spin. She grabbed her tablet from her bag and sat in the comfortable chair in the corner. She searched online for any part-time employment in the area. She jotted down a couple possibilities and then pulled up her gallery of photos. Tears filled her dark eyes as she scrolled through memories.

Her finger stopped on a photo of a young woman, smiling in front of a beautiful arch surrounded by trees. A fat teardrop fell on the screen. Hope wiped a finger beneath her eye and ran her sleeve across the tablet. "Good night my sweet girl."

6

Tuesday morning Jake woke early, got himself ready, ate breakfast, and put Scout's harness on so she would be set for their outing. Hope warned him to do as Drew said and pay attention during the walk so he would know how to handle Scout. He and the dog stood at the back door watching and waiting. True to his word, Drew arrived with Dickens and Fletch and set off down the road with his young admirer holding Scout's leash.

Hope visited with the only couple in residence while she served them leftover casserole and blueberry scones. Anxious to get to their son's house, they left as soon as they finished the meal.

Hope delivered breakfast to Dottie and then dashed upstairs to get the couple's room straightened. Once done, she went about stripping and disinfecting the Blue Room and moved their things to the guest bedroom in Dottie's wing. Dottie's home care nurse, Beth, arrived at the same time Jake and Drew returned.

Hope and Jake enticed the dogs with some treats and let Drew and Dottie speak with Beth. Hope went about cleaning the kitchen and studied the recipe for tomorrow's breakfast while Jake played with the dogs.

Soon Drew emerged and strode to the kitchen. "Jake did a fine job with the dogs. I showed him the trail to take, so he should be good to take Scout on her walks. She's a good girl and doesn't stray or pull on the leash. She knows the way."

"I'll try to go with him one afternoon, so I know where he'll be walking." She turned to the fridge. "There's enough breakfast for you, if you'd like it."

He glanced at his watch with impatience. "I'll have to hurry. I'm on the verge of being late now."

She put together a plate, and he sipped coffee while he waited. "Mom likes the nurse. She'll be by again on Friday since Thursday is a holiday." She set the plate in front of him, and he dug into a quick meal.

Minutes later, the plate was clean and the cup empty. "I've got to get to the office. I'm already behind." He hollered out for the dogs, and they came running, followed by Jake.

Determined to show Drew kindness, she wished him a good day and gathered his dirty dishes. Jake petted the dogs on the head and waved goodbye as they hopped in Drew's SUV. Hope guided her son back to the kitchen where she went to work at the sink. She quizzed him on his spelling words while they waited for the nurse to finish her visit. In the midst of their lesson, Scout barreled through the kitchen and stationed herself at the backdoor.

Grant's bakery van rolled to a stop near Scout's lookout position. He gathered boxes and Hope helped him bring in the groceries. He showed Hope where to store things before hurrying to get back to the bakery.

Beth said goodbye on her way out the door, as Jake and Scout rushed down the hall to Dottie's family room. The nurse had helped Dottie shower and put on fresh clothes. She was back in her recliner, the television muted.

"I'm worn out," she said with a sigh. "Felt good to have a shower, but dear me, I'm tired."

"I'll read to you, and you can take a nap," offered Jake, choosing a book from his stash.

She smiled and said, "That sounds like a grand idea." Scout plopped onto the floor at Dottie's side and shut her eyes.

Before Jake started his story, he filled Dottie in on his morning adventure with Drew and the dogs. Hope left a couple of his workbooks on the coffee table and pointed at them. Jake nodded his understanding as he turned to the first page of his book.

Hope finished getting the Blue Room ready for the guests who would be arriving tomorrow. Once finished, she popped in to check on Jake, who was still babbling and reading to Dottie. Her eyes fluttered shut, and Hope retreated without interrupting.

Hope needed bacon for the breakfast recipe she'd be making tomorrow. Dottie had shared her secret of baking it in the oven, so she spread out the slices on a sheet and placed it in the oven. She inventoried the cookies and snacks in the freezer and unearthed a container to thaw for tomorrow.

She organized the ingredients for tomorrow's breakfast and put away the remaining supplies Grant had delivered. Once the bacon was done, she checked on Jake, who was busy working in his workbooks while Dottie dozed in her chair.

Hope fixed a cup of tea, snagged one of the fresh pumpkin cookies she had found in the freezer, stoked the fire, and sat down for a well-deserved break. She used her cell phone to call one of the businesses advertising for seasonal help. Disappointed after a short conversation, she disconnected. The hours for the job conflicted with her helping Dottie.

She took a deep breath and another bite of cookie. She shut her eyes for a few minutes. She woke with a start when she heard the click of toenails from sixteen additional paws coming through the house. Her eyes struggled to focus as she looked at the clock.

She shot from the chair, cheeks crimson with embarrassment. She had slept for over two hours, and it was after five. She heard the deep voices of Grant and Drew from the kitchen, commanding the dogs. In a blur, Jake and Scout scurried by on their way to the kitchen.

She took a deep breath and ran her hands through her hair. She stepped into the kitchen and went about helping to get the leftovers heated and the table set. Drew escorted Dottie, who took her seat at the table looking more alert and well-rested than she had for a couple of days. Beth suggested she use a walker since the crutches had been difficult. Dottie's confidence and steadiness had improved with the addition of the new contraption.

The dinner discussion centered around Thanksgiving. Grant would be taking up residence in the kitchen starting tomorrow afternoon. Drew was closing the office early and would take care of picking up something for dinner and be around to help with whatever was needed.

Grant was making the pies and rolls at the bakery and bringing them to Dottie's to cook. He was brining the turkey at his house and would bring it over to roast on Thursday morning. Drew's contributions included a bit of labor and a check to cover the costs of the meal.

Hope listened as they discussed the dishes Grant would be cooking, based on Dottie's menu. "I'm happy to help with anything. Just give me an assignment," said Hope, pouring another glass of water.

"I'll take you up on that offer. I could use all the help I can get," said Grant. "Mom can supervise."

She smiled. "I trust you completely. I'll watch over Jake while you two handle dinner."

As soon as the dinner mess was cleaned up, Hope gave Jake a bath and wished the family a pleasant evening. She was exhausted and knew the next five days would have her running from sunup to sundown.

Wednesday morning Hope crept out of bed and started her kitchen tasks early. She put together the blueberry breakfast cake and got it in the oven. While that was baking, she mixed the ingredients for the bacon, egg, and cheese bake. The kitchen smelled heavenly. She fixed a cup of tea and started a fire before settling into a comfortable chair.

The house was quiet, save for the crackling of the logs and the errant chirp from a visiting bird. Memories of past Thanksgivings flooded her mind. She shook her head, widened her eyes to stave off tears, and focused her gaze on the orange flames licking around the dark wood.

She had to find a job that would allow her to work in the evenings for a few hours. She knew Dottie would watch over Jake if she found something that would work. Her duties at the guest house took up most of the morning, and she needed to be around for check-ins later in the afternoon. She hated to share her dilemma with Dottie, who Hope suspected would renew the offer to pay her for her work.

The buzzer sounded from the oven, and she retrieved the blueberry treat that looked more appropriate for dessert than breakfast. She slid in the egg dish and set the timer. The aroma of sugar and blueberries wafted through the downstairs.

She had stashed her things in the bathroom off the mudroom last night. She didn't want to wake Jake or Dottie any earlier than necessary. She slipped inside and started the shower. Minutes later, she emerged dressed with her hair still wet in time to retrieve breakfast from the oven.

She left it to cool on the counter and started the coffee brewing. She made sure the table was set for the guests and indulged in breakfast alone while she waited for the household to wake. She plucked a book from the library under the staircase to keep her company. She escaped with a mystery while she ate the delicious meal. She giggled when she remembered Dottie told her she liked to sample everything before the guests ate it.

The aroma of fresh coffee worked its magic and soon the couple from upstairs descended. They complimented Hope on the meal and chatted about their Thanksgiving plans.

When they finished and were lingering at the table with coffee, Hope excused herself to check on Jake. He was awake, but still in bed. She whispered, "Good morning. Are you hungry?"

He nodded and stretched. "Let's get you dressed. We need to be quiet, so we don't wake Dottie." She helped him find his clothes, and as they were tiptoeing through the family room, she heard noise from Dottie's room.

She poked her head in, and Dottie gave her a wave. "Are you ready for breakfast?" asked Hope.

"When you get time. No hurry. Coffee would be wonderful." Dottie smiled at the pair of them. "Smells delicious."

Hope gave her a smile and said, "I had some already, and I must say it was great. I'll have to remember those recipes."

Scout accompanied them to the kitchen and Jake scooped her breakfast into her bowl while Hope made him a plate. She delivered a tray to Dottie and ran into the couple on her way back to the kitchen. They wished her a good day and said they would be late tonight.

She sat with Jake while he ate and they planned to take

Scout for a walk together as soon as she did her upstairs chores. Jake visited with Dottie while Hope took care of the couple's room.

They left Dottie with the television on and took off down the road with Scout. The fresh scent of pine punctuated the crisp morning air. Scout knew her way and led them down the trail. They had taken a different way from the house but ended up at the lake, following Drew's route.

The mountains behind the lake were capped with snow. The morning light danced across the top of the water. Hope retrieved her phone to take a picture. She had been so intent on skipping rocks during their last visit, she hadn't taken in the scenery.

The slap of the water against the shore, the chirping of the birds, and the chatter of squirrels were the only sounds. Peace. Hope felt at peace here. She kept her eye on Scout and Jake who were drifting between the shoreline and the trees beyond the beach. Scout had her nose to the ground, and Jake was babbling to her.

Despite the clear blue sky and the bright sun, Hope's hands were getting cold. She hollered at Jake and Scout led him to her. "We better get going, buddy. It's cold." She had them pose for a few pictures together in front of the water.

They joined the road they had used before and wandered past the RV park. "Now if you come by yourself with Scout, no stopping at the lake. I need to be with you if you're near the water. Scout needs to keep moving for exercise, so you just follow the road back to the house. Okay, Jake?"

He was hurrying after Scout and nodded, but she made him vocalize his understanding of the rules. "You have to do as I say, or no walking Scout."

"Yes, Mom." She couldn't see them but knew his eyes would be rolling with annoyance.

She jogged to catch up to the dog and took the leash to set

the pace. Jake chattered on the trip home asking questions about where the water came from for the lake. She answered what she could and promised they would make it a school project to investigate the area and learn all they could about the mountains, rivers, and lakes in the area.

"I'll ask Dottie about a library and see if we can find some books to help us learn about Silver Falls."

They had a quick lunch before Drew and Grant arrived with the dogs. Hope gave Jake the afternoon off from school, and he entertained the dogs on the back lawn. Grant got to work in the kitchen while Drew helped his mom move out to the main living room.

Soon the guests arrived, and Hope kept busy checking them in. Drew helped with their luggage and showed them to their rooms. Once she had all the paperwork completed, she abandoned the desk to check on Jake. She found him sitting at the counter munching on a snack and chatting with Grant.

"Oh, sorry. I got swamped," she said.

"Not to worry. Jake and I are solving the world's problems." Grant smiled and went about chopping.

She took a platter of cookies and brownies and placed them in the living room, giving Dottie first choice. Soon the guests filtered downstairs and helped themselves to the treats and hot drinks. They visited until the dinner hour and then went on their way to visit family or a restaurant.

Drew made sure the dogs were fed. Soon after their dinner, the pack of furry friends collapsed in front of the fire, exhausted from the hours of running with Jake. "How do you feel about pizza, Jake?"

The boy's eyes twinkled. "I loooove pizza."

"It should be here in a few minutes." Drew gathered paper

plates and stationed them on the table before helping his mother navigate to the dining area. Pumpkin and apple pies were baking in the oven, filling the house with the inviting scents of cinnamon and warm sugar.

Grant was busy putting together an overnight casserole for tomorrow's breakfast. Dottie was at the table, taking in the activities and petting Scout, who had left the other dogs snoozing to be near Dottie.

The doorbell sounded, and Jake scrambled to his feet and ran to the door. All the dogs were rousted and clamored to follow him. Drew hurried to the door and returned holding three pizza boxes high in the air, out of reach of the curious dogs.

He placed the boxes on the table and herded the dogs to the mudroom, giving them a quick command. They plopped onto their beds, and he rewarded them with treats.

Grant retrieved his pies before joining the rest of them for slices of pizza. Jake ate three huge slices of pizza. Hope noticed his eyelids getting heavier. She finished her last slice and excused both of them. "We're going to call it a night. See you in the morning."

They said their goodnights and Grant added, "Don't worry about getting up early for breakfast duty. I'll be here and take care of it."

Hope bundled Jake into bed and slipped into the matching twin bed. The exhaustion from the day was a welcome respite from the constant worry about the car repair. Her mind gave up and sleep replaced the lack of solutions that occupied her thoughts each night.

7

Hope woke before five the next morning. She wrapped herself in her robe and tiptoed through the house and out to the kitchen. She brewed a cup of tea and held the warm ceramic in her hands to warm them.

She grabbed a notepad and wrote down the two figures Chet had provided. She subtracted the money she could spare from her savings and circled the remaining amounts. She knew she couldn't make much per hour working odd jobs, so she calculated a conservative amount.

Once she did that, she divided the large number by her hourly rate and gasped when she saw the number of hours she'd have to work. She rested her elbow on the table and cupped her forehead with her hand.

The sound of the back door startled her. She made her way to the mudroom and saw Grant propping the door open, so he could muscle the turkey into the house. He turned and said, "Whoa, I didn't expect anyone to be up. It's so early."

She shrugged. "Couldn't sleep." She held the door and said, "Let me help you."

He toted the electric roaster into the kitchen and went about getting it set up for cooking. Hope took in the scent of herbs and lemon and said, "Smells good already."

Once he had it going, he started the coffee brewing. Hope refilled her tea and sat back down at the table. She heard kitchen sounds as Grant staged pans on the cooktop and retrieved ingredients from the fridge.

The rich aroma of fresh coffee filled the kitchen, and a few minutes later Grant slid into a chair across from Hope. He glanced at the notepad and saw rows of numbers. "Whatcha working on?"

She turned the pad over. "Just figuring out how I'm going to pay for the transmission. I need to find a job."

"Seems to me you have a job. Right here." He gestured his hand to the kitchen.

"I'm helping Dottie in exchange for room and board. I need to find something to augment the meager savings I can contribute. Something in the evenings when I'm not needed here."

She told him about her search and the paltry results. He frowned and said, "This is probably the best time of year to find seasonal work. All the shops are busy with the upcoming Festival of Lights."

She gave him a quizzical look. He went on to explain the festival started the day after Thanksgiving with a huge tree lighting downtown. All the shops decorated with lights. Homeowners went all out and decorated entire neighborhoods. Churches, the park, and the gazebo were lit up in celebration of the season. Each weekend there was a special event. Choral recitals, cookie exchanges, a torchlight parade at the ski lodge, and fireworks were planned.

"Who should I talk to?" asked Hope, with a spark of enthusiasm. "They don't have them advertised."

He nodded. "Most of them go to people who've always

had the jobs. It's word of mouth for the most part." He took a sip of coffee. "Tell you what. I need some help at the bakery. With the upcoming events, we're super busy. I could give you some work cleaning up each evening and doing some of the prep for the morning."

"That sounds terrific. If I can get your mom to keep an eye on Jake. I figure I can start anytime around five or six after check-ins are done here."

"I'm flexible. I'll give you a key, and you can come in whenever it works. I'll show you the ropes this weekend. I'm sure Mom would be happy to watch Jake."

The strain of worry evaporated from Hope's face, leaving only a smile and her bright eyes. "You don't know how much I appreciate this."

"Don't give it a thought. It's a win-win." He gave her a wink. "I better get back in the kitchen."

"I'll run and get ready and help you." She sprang from her chair and followed him.

"I've got a bag of potatoes with your name on it," he said in a loud whisper as she hurried past the island.

The guests enjoyed Grant's pecan French toast bake but were eager to begin their holiday festivities and left after breakfast. Drew arrived as they were leaving. He and his dogs came through the back door, where Scout was ready to greet them.

After Hope peeled all the potatoes, she checked on Jake and Dottie. She helped both of them get ready and get to the table. The family, along with Jake and Hope, ate breakfast together after the guests were gone.

Drew addressed Jake from across the table. "How about helping me with the tree today?"

The boy's eyes went wide, and his mouth formed an open oval. "Wow, really? Today?"

"We always put our tree up while the turkey is cooking. There's a huge Christmas celebration in town, and we run out of time if we wait." Drew explained the Festival of Lights, sharing what Grant had described to Hope earlier in the morning.

As Drew talked, Jake vibrated with excitement and a goofy smile filled his face. "This is going to be our best Christmas ever," he shouted.

Hope shook her head and laughed. "Okay, buddy, calm down. You've still got your schoolwork to get done, and we have to help Dottie. You'll have to behave and do all your work if you want to go to the celebrations."

His body stilled, and he gave his mother a serious look. "I'll behave, Mom. I promise."

"Let's get started on the tree. We'll put it out front in the living room. I'll drive the truck around there, and it'll make it easier."

Grant stood, "I'll help you get it in. Then you and Jake can handle the rest of it."

Their decades of experience in the tree installation process paid off, and the two sons had it up in no time. Dottie sat on the couch by the fire and directed the placement and had Hope fetch more decorations.

For the next couple of hours, Hope and Jake helped Drew drape the lights. Drew wouldn't let anyone else on the ladder and had them hand him the ornaments for the top third of the tree. He watched as Hope and Jake finished adding ornaments to the lower portions, while Dottie chimed in with suggestions. Grant took a break from the kitchen and went home to retrieve his dogs.

Dottie watched from the window as he drove down the driveway. "Poor Grant. He's been working nonstop since the breakup. I don't think this Thanksgiving will be easy on him. Not with Curt being gone and his girlfriend Lisa having moved across the country a couple of months ago."

"Oh, that's too bad," said Hope.

Dottie went on to explain Grant and Lisa had been in a serious relationship for several years. "Lisa put in for a job and was surprised to get it. She hadn't told Grant about the job search and expected him to give up his business and move with her. It ended in a mess. I don't think he's dealing with it. Just working himself to death to avoid it." Dottie shook her head.

Drew clapped his hands together, and the lounging dogs came to attention. "How about we take these scoundrels outside and run around. Luna and Ginger will be here in a few minutes, and they can all play together."

Jake jumped at the chance and ran to find his coat. He herded the dogs outside onto the porch and to the lawn. Dottie laughed when she saw them all tumble together in a heap.

"I wish I had a tenth of his energy," said Dottie with a chuckle. She watched Drew toss a toy to the dogs and Jake scramble to try to get it. "I didn't want to say this in front of Drew, but I'm afraid Grant is following in his big brother's footsteps. Drew withdrew from life when he lost Danny and Laura. It almost ended him." She used her walker and eased into her chair. "Not to say it's the same. Just a sense of loss. Grant isn't handling it well. Drew still struggles. Now without Curt, it's even harder."

Hope handed her a tissue and patted her hand. "I'm sorry, Dottie. I know how hard loss can be. I can also see how much you mean to your sons. It's wonderful that you all live so close and are there for each other."

Dottie's head bobbed as she dabbed at the tears on her

cheeks. "That is so true. I'd be lost without them. Sometimes I just get a bit weepy and feel sorry for myself."

Hope smiled. "You're entitled." They heard Drew and Jake laughing and shouting. "We've been cooped up in the car most days, so this is good for him to be able to run around. I can't say I'm happy the car broke down, but if it had to quit on us, I'm glad it happened here. I appreciate you taking us in."

"My dear, like I said when you arrived, you're here for a reason. I'm thankful you're here right now. There's no way I could keep up with this place without you."

Hope told her about Grant's offer of work in the evenings. "I did the math this morning, and it's going to take me two months of part-time work to get the repair paid for at Chet's."

Dottie listened while Hope asked her about watching over Jake in the evenings. Hope would make sure he had a bath and was set for bed before she left. She just needed someone to keep him company and make him go to bed on time.

"Sounds like a perfect trade to me. It'll calm down starting next week, but the weekends will be busy because of the festival."

"Grant is flexible on my hours, so we'll play it by ear here, and if it gets to be too much, I'll limit my time to the weekday evenings only."

"I'm sure we can make it work. Drew comes over in the evenings, and he can help with anything I need here. Scout and Jake and I will be fine."

The noise outside increased as Luna and Ginger arrived and joined the circus act in progress on the front lawn. Dottie opted for a nap while Hope helped Grant with the rest of the meal preparation.

The five humans enjoyed a delicious Thanksgiving dinner, and the five dogs slept after getting a few bites of turkey added to their evening kibble. Drew insisted on doing the dishes and Grant relaxed next to the fire and visited with his mom. Hope ushered Jake to the guest bath and made sure he was clean before getting him into his pajamas.

Once the kitchen chores were done, Drew joined them, and Grant served pie to the group while they settled in to watch *Grumpy Old Men*. It had been one of Curt's favorite traditions during the holiday. The television in the living room area wasn't usually on, as it was reserved for the guests, but tonight Dottie made an exception.

The lights from the tree and the flame from the fire provided the perfect cozy feel for relaxing. Jake fell asleep snuggled up next to Hope, and she watched the threesome laugh at the funny lines in the movie, commenting on Curt's favorite parts. Amid the laughter, Hope saw tears on Dottie's face and noticed the boys wipe their eyes a few times. Memories, comforting and painful at the same time, triggered powerful emotions.

Hope rose early the next morning and found Grant and Drew sprawled on the couches in Dottie's family room. She tiptoed down the hall to the kitchen to get breakfast started for the guests.

Keeping in mind the large meals eaten last night, Dottie always planned a light breakfast for guests the morning after Thanksgiving. Hope started the water boiling for the steel cut oats and washed berries. She organized yogurt cups in an ice bowl and got the coffee brewing.

There were a few leftover pastries that could be eaten and fresh bread for toast. She made sure plates and utensils were stacked and ready. While the oats simmered, she fixed a cup of tea and wandered into the living room. She plugged in the lights and burrowed under a blanket.

Memories of the holidays flooded her mind. The colored lights twinkled and then blurred. Doubts about her decision to take Jake on a road trip adventure swirled amid her recollections of past Christmas celebrations. The game she was playing was risky.

She reached for a tissue and wiped her eyes. She flinched at the sound of a soft scuffle. Turning she saw Grant as he made his way to the kitchen. He joined her a few minutes later, holding a cup of coffee.

"Are you okay?" he asked. "What's wrong?"

She swallowed hard and said, "Just the holidays stirring up memories. I'm fine."

"I understand. This year is hard without Dad." He took a sip from his cup. "It's my first year without Lisa, my girlfriend. We broke up a couple of months ago."

Hope didn't divulge her knowledge of his situation. "Oh, I'm so sorry. That can't be easy for you. Change is difficult." Her gaze returned to the lights on the tree.

She listened as he explained his girlfriend's departure and new job. "I'm still feeling betrayed. I never thought she'd go behind my back like that, or just leave." He shook his head. "Good thing I'm too busy to think about it much."

Hope smiled as she stood. "I know the feeling." She offered to refill his cup as she made her way to the kitchen to check on breakfast. She stirred the oats and set them aside to keep warm.

She refilled their cups and tiptoed back to the living room. He took the cup from her and said, "You don't have to answer this, but we get the feeling you're running from something. Are you okay? I'm only asking out of our concern for you."

Her throat tightened. "I appreciate the concern. I, um, just ——", she was interrupted by the pounding of feet and the click of nails on the wood as Jake slid into the room followed by five dogs.

"Mommy, Mommy, the dogs are chasing me," he said with a squeal.

"Shhh, be quieter, we don't want to wake the guests." She shook her head and grabbed the boy when he got close to the chair. "Are you ready for some breakfast?"

He nodded and laughed as the dogs surrounded them, Scout licking his arm.

"I better get these wild animals their breakfast," Grant said, moaning as he rose from the couch. "I'm sure glad the bakery is closed today. I'm beat."

He went about dispensing dog food, while Hope breathed a sigh of relief and kissed Jake on top of his head. "Let's get you something to eat. Then we'll get our chores done and get ready for the town tree lighting tonight."

That was all it took to keep Jake motivated all day. He ate breakfast, dressed and brushed his teeth, and helped Hope with the dishes after all the guests had eaten and left for the day. He followed her as she went about spiffing up the guest rooms and retrieved items she needed.

With the tasks done for the day, they wandered back downstairs in search of a snack. "Mmm," said Hope. "Something smells delicious in here."

Grant, Drew, and Dottie were sitting at the dining table. "It's some turkey chili I put in the slow cooker. We can have it tonight after the tree lighting," said Grant.

"He just put some bread in the oven," said Dottie. "We were just discussing lunch."

Hope helped Grant put together some turkey sandwiches

and fruit. "I was going to offer to make some soup this weekend. I've got a great recipe for a Greek lemon chicken soup, and it works well with turkey," said Hope, carrying the plate of sandwiches to the table.

"Sounds delicious," said Dottie. "Let's plan on your soup for Sunday, and we'll eat up more of the leftovers tomorrow night."

"Tomorrow is the scavenger hunt and choral competition, and we'll be busy, so leftovers will be great," said Grant. "Speaking of work, after lunch we can run down to the bakery, and I'll walk you through your tasks. I need to get some things started this afternoon, so you can help with that and then start your cleaning routine tomorrow."

While they discussed logistics, Jake peppered Drew and Dottie with questions about the tree lighting and the scavenger hunt. Once they finished lunch, Hope and Jake piled into Grant's truck and he drove them downtown to the bakery.

Jake wandered looking at the empty cases, taking in the view from the large windows facing Main Street. He settled into one of the bench seats along the wall and rested against the colorful pillows that were stacked against the wooden seat. He rifled in his backpack for some schoolwork.

"What a great space you have," said Hope. She marveled at the rustic shop, decorated with lots of dark wood and accents of black and white. The glass display cases were spotless, and the marble counters gleamed.

Grant prepared a small plate of cookies and a glass of milk and gave them to Jake. He flicked the switch to turn on the pendulum lights that hung over the seating area, so Jake could see his papers and books. "There you go, buddy. We'll be back in the kitchen area if you need anything."

He put together the ingredients for his dough and went about getting pans ready for bread. He had Hope measure ingredients and dump them into the large bowl of the commercial floor mixer. He finished off the cookie dough and put it in the cooler to chill.

They worked for hours and made muffins and brownies and several batches of cookies while the bread rose. Hope took a break to check on Jake and found him curled up, surrounded by the pillows, fast asleep.

They continued their work while the delightful aroma of baked goods filled the air. The tree lighting was scheduled for six o'clock and as the sky darkened, the streets filled with townspeople and visitors. They had just finished the last of the dishes when they heard the side door open and saw Drew helping Dottie.

Grant hurried to hold the door and help his mom to a table. The commotion woke Jake who smiled when he saw Dottie sitting at the table next to his. "Are you ready for the tree ceremony?" she asked.

He spun around to look out the window. "Is it starting?"

Grant placed a plate of fresh cookies on the table as Dottie explained they still had about thirty minutes to wait. Hope made sure the kitchen was clean and everything was put away and joined Jake.

Drew took another cookie and passed one to his mom. "So how was the lesson tonight?" she asked.

Hope smiled and nodded. "It was good. I helped Grant with some of the prep, and I think I have a good grip on what needs to be done after closing. Her eyes widened, and she dangled a key in front of them. "He gave me a key to the place, so I guess I passed."

Dottie chuckled. "Sounds like you're official." She reached for another cookie. "These are delicious, but I need to stop eating them." She elected to stay indoors and watch the tree from the window, and Grant offered to stay with her.

Drew, Hope, and Jake braved the crowded sidewalks to

get a closer view. A band was playing carols, and they watched as a man approached an elevated platform in front of the tree. Drew bent down and said, "That man is Mayor Douglas. He's going to start the ceremony."

Jake tugged on Hope's coat. "I can't see."

Drew scooped Jake up and put him on his shoulders. "How's that?"

"Wow, I can see everything." Jake's shoes beat against Drew's coat, and Hope raised her hand and stopped the movement.

"Sit still up there. Drew doesn't need you wiggling around." Her eyes met Drew's. "Thanks for hoisting him up there."

"No problem. I used to do this all the time …with Danny."

Her hand slipped off Jake's shoe, and with a slight hesitation, she placed it on top of Drew's. "Grant told me about him. I know the words seem hollow, but I am very sorry."

Drew's eyes clouded and he nodded. The carol ended, and Mayor Douglas tapped the microphone. "Ladies and gentleman. Boys and girls. Welcome to the eighty-fourth annual Silver Falls Tree Lighting Celebration."

He introduced several people and then revved up the crowd by having them countdown from ten and pushed the giant red plunger when the crowd yelled the last number. The dark tree was awash in lights. The crowd gasped and clapped at the sight of the huge tree, decked out in thousands of festive lights.

Moments later, both sides of the street came alive with lights adorning all the shopfronts. The small trees and lampposts lining both sides of the street were draped with fresh greenery and huge red bows. White twinkly lights adorned all the trees making for a postcard worthy scene.

Hope's eyes filled with tears when she saw the happiness radiating from Jake's face. It was like standing in the midst of a Christmas village. Mayor Douglas announced Santa was spotted and would soon be arriving to take his place of honor in a giant velvet chair placed next to the tree.

The children in the crowd rushed to form a line to meet Santa. Jake shouted, "Mommy, Santa is coming. You didn't tell me he'd be here. Can I go see him?"

She chuckled and said, "Yes, you can go see him. I didn't know he was coming either."

Drew helped him wriggle off his shoulders and planted him on the ground in front of Hope. "It's safe to let him stand in line. You can watch from the side."

She nodded her thanks and took Jake's hand to lead him to the line of anxious children. A roar of excitement announced the arrival of Santa in a horse-drawn carriage. He bellowed a "Ho, ho, ho," and took his seat, asking the first child to step forward.

Cameras flashed as children posed for pictures and told Santa their secret wishes. Drew handed Hope a cup of hot chocolate and she sipped it as she watched Jake inch closer to the man with the realistic long white beard.

She pulled her phone from her pocket and snapped several pictures of him sitting on Santa's lap. When he was done sharing his Christmas list, he posed in front of the tree for her. She gripped his hand in hers, and they walked through the crowd. Excitement oozed from every pore of his body. He chattered nonstop about Santa and his reindeer and the softness of his red suit.

She led him back to the bakery where she found the others waiting. Jake insisted on repeating his experience for Dottie, and she listened with rapt attention. Grant and Drew let Jake finish his long-winded recounting before suggesting they get home and have dinner.

She and Jake rode with Grant and Drew drove his mother. The dogs greeted them at the door. The smell of

Grant's chili beckoned them to the kitchen. Hope helped Grant get bowls of chili and slices of his fresh baked bread on the table.

As soon as they were finished, Hope cleared the table. "We're going to call it a night. Tomorrow is a big day with some guests leaving. The others need their linens changed." She patted Jake on the head. "This one is worn out from the excitement of the tree."

Jake gave Scout a snuggle, and she ended up following them to the guest room. Hope slipped into bed and didn't hear the conversation in the kitchen.

"She's such a hard-working young woman," said Dottie. "We're lucky she's here."

"I agree," added Grant. "I admire her for being willing to take a cleaning job to earn the money she needs."

Drew sighed. "That's all well and good, but there's something amiss with her. Something she's not telling us."

8

Saturday morning brought a flurry of activity. Hope kept busy from the time she rose until mid-afternoon. The guests in the Blue Room checked out, so she was able to move their things back into it, once she finished cleaning.

Jake's patience was wearing thin. Hope promised to take him to town to watch the choral competition. The scavenger hunt involved visiting and shopping at the stores on Main Street. She explained they didn't have extra money to spend while she was saving for the transmission repair.

Dottie did her best to appease him and told him he could get a treat from the bakery while he listened to the choirs sing. "It's more fun than running around to stores. That's boring."

Hope zipped up Jake's coat and made him put on his hat and gloves. "It's cold, and we have a long walk."

Dottie overheard her and said, "Just take my car. You'll spend all your time walking, and you've worked nonstop today." She explained her keys were hanging on the peg by the door in the mudroom. "Just click the button to open the garage door."

"Oh, I hate to borrow your car. I don't want to be responsible for it. We can walk or ride our bikes."

Dottie waved her hand. "Don't be silly. It's just a car. Nothing's going to happen. Just take it. Park in back of the bakery or at Drew's veterinary office. There's parking in the back of it, if it's too busy on the street."

Hope did her best to resist, but Dottie persevered and insisted she take the car. After buckling Jake in, she eased the car out of the garage and steered for town. She slipped into a spot behind the bakery.

She and Jake wandered down the street and heard the singing near the tree. Jake tugged on her coat and motioned to the bakery. She opened the door, and they waited in a long line. Grant looked up from the counter and gestured them to the end of the counter. He snagged a tray of cookies from the kitchen and presented it to them.

Jake's eyes brightened, and he looked at his mother for permission. She nodded her head, and he took two cookies from the tray. She selected one for herself and thanked Grant.

"We've been swamped all day long. It's been a zoo." He looked back at the line.

"I promised Jake we'd come check out the activities. Your mom let us borrow her car."

"Makes sense. She can't use it, somebody might as well drive it. You can drive it down here in the evenings when you're working."

She shook her head. "Really, I can ride my bike."

Jake was in a hurry to get outside, so she didn't have time to argue the point. In the end, she agreed to consider the use of Dottie's car. "I just don't want Drew to get upset. I sense he doesn't trust me."

Grant laughed. "He doesn't trust anyone. Don't worry

about him." He promised to see her tonight for dinner and hurried to get back to work.

She and Jake found seats on a bench near the choir and helped themselves to free hot chocolates from a young man in an elf costume. They listened to several groups sing holiday tunes and ate their cookies.

As dusk settled in, the lights along the street became vibrant. When Hope gave Jake the eye and tapped her watch, he begged to listen to one more song. She agreed but made him traverse the sidewalk and head back toward the car as they listened to the end of the piece. He had his ballot ready with his favorite groups marked and dropped it in the collection bin before they rounded the corner.

They made it back to Dottie's and found Drew in the kitchen. It was his night to be in charge of dinner. Dottie was stationed in the dining room, supervising the process of heating leftovers. Hope returned the keys to the peg in the mudroom and thanked her for the use of her car.

"You can use it when you go to work at the bakery. It's too late at night to be riding your bike into town, not to mention the time it would take."

Hope saw Drew's brow furrow. He remained silent. He didn't have to say anything. His disapproving look spoke for him.

Hope whisked Jake away to get him ready for bed and left Dottie alone with Drew. As she opened the door to the Blue Room, she heard their muffled conversation. She told Jake to get his pajamas out and head for the bathtub. She tiptoed back down the hallway and listened.

She heard Dottie's loud whisper. "I told you, she's perfectly trustworthy. She's leaving her son with me for goodness sake, what do you think she's going to do, run off in my car?"

In a gruff voice, Drew said, "There's just something she's

hiding. I don't want you to be taken advantage of by some stranger. I'm just trying to protect you, Mom."

Hope stretched and bent as far as she dared, but couldn't make out any more of the conversation. She scuttled back to the room and helped Jake. Grant joined them for an early dinner that was every bit as delicious as the original Thanksgiving meal they shared.

Jake was already in his pajamas at the dinner table, and the frown on his face advertised his displeasure. "As soon as we're done with dinner, I'm going to get my pajamas on," said Dottie. "We can sit by the fire, and you can read to me and Scout. Then we'll have some popcorn."

Jake's frown disappeared, and he gave Dottie a sweet smile. Hope started to clear the dishes when Grant said, "You leave all this to us. Go ahead and get a start at the bakery."

Hope gave Jake a kiss goodbye and promised to be home soon. She parked behind the bakery and used her key to access the back door. She went about her duties and listened to the singing still going on outside. She used the checklist Grant had left to make sure she had completed everything before shutting out the lights for the night.

She admired the soft glow of colored lights reflecting off the bakery window as she left for the evening. She arrived back at Dottie's and found Jake snuggled in their bed, fast asleep. Grant had left, but Drew was still there visiting with Dottie.

She poked her head into the family room and wished them both a good night before heading to bed.

Sunday, Hope was up early getting things organized for breakfast when Grant arrived with the morning delivery. He put the box on the counter and said, "I'm usually closed on

Sundays, but during the festival, we're so busy it pays to stay open."

They chatted while she finished the meal and put a casserole in the oven. "We don't have any guests booked in for tomorrow or the next day, so I'll have some extra time."

"Come on down early, and you can help with some of the prep for baking. I can use all the help I can get, so feel free to come whenever it works." He finished his coffee and headed back to work.

The guests were checking out today and were up early to eat and hit the road. As soon as they left, Hope looked in on Dottie and found Jake visiting with her in the family room. "Are you two ready for breakfast?"

Jake gave her an enthusiastic nod and hopped off the couch. Dottie smiled and said, "Drew is on his way."

Hope stiffened her spine and made her way to the kitchen. She set the table and heard the scuffle of dogs and knew Drew had arrived. Having eaten with the guests, Hope excused herself to get started on their rooms while Dottie and Drew ate and watched over Jake.

By the time she was done with the rooms, Jake was outside with Drew and the dogs. She paused and took in the scene from the window. Drew's relaxed smile and Jake's constant laughter trumpeted their genuine happiness. The dogs ran circles around the two humans as they raced to fetch balls.

The sternness and doubt Drew displayed with Hope vanished when he was with Jake. She continued to watch as the man and boy bonded through their shared love of play and dogs.

The weekdays were calm and relaxed at the guest house. She and Jake spent time each day walking Scout and exploring the lake. With Dottie's guidance, they baked cookies and brownies to restock the freezer.

Without many guests during the week, Hope was able to go to the bakery early and put in a few more hours. Friday morning dawned and with it came the realization of a busy weekend.

Hope got up early to organize the day, as four couples would be arriving to stay the weekend. She stoked the fire on her way to the kitchen. When she turned and looked out the window, she did a double take. The light from the porch illuminated gentle flakes of snow falling from the sky.

She smiled knowing how excited Jake would be to see the snow. Tomorrow was the torchlight parade on the ski mountain and Hope had promised Jake they would go. She went about her prep work, and when the household woke, she heard Jake thunder down the hall.

"It's snowing. It's snowing. I wanna go out and play. Can I, Mommy?"

Hope made sure he ate breakfast and helped him put on his hat and gloves before she released him to the outdoors. Scout followed, and the two of them romped in the snow for much of the day.

Once Hope had all the guests checked in Friday, she joined the others for dinner. Grant had made a hearty meat-loaf with all the trimmings. The chatter around the table involved snow and the upcoming parade on the mountain.

As she listened to the excited voice of her son, Hope's eyes began to close. She was jostled from her drowsy state with Drew's voice. "Hope, are you okay?"

She focused her eyes and said, "I, uh, don't feel so great." She put her hand to her throat. "My throat really hurts."

Drew stood and placed a hand on Hope's forehead. "You're pretty warm." He felt her neck and added, "Swollen glands."

Dottie flashed a look of concern. "Let's get her to bed. She needs to rest."

Drew helped Hope to her room. Grant followed with a tray of tea, juice, and water. "You get some sleep, and we'll check on you later," said Drew.

Dottie and Jake finished their dinner, and while they were chatting, Dottie suggested he have a camp out in her wing of the house. "You can build a blanket fort and sleep with Scout tonight."

Jake fidgeted in his chair. His enthusiasm for the idea evident in his exaggerated nods and smiles. When Drew and Grant returned from getting Hope settled, she asked them to fetch extra sheets and blankets and show Jake how to construct a fort in her living room.

The brothers sported wide grins as they led Jake down the hallway. Over the next couple of hours, they worked and made a huge blanket fort, decorated with multi-colored twinkle lights. They found an old sleeping bag and stacked tons of pillows inside so Jake and Scout would be comfortable and warm.

Once they had Jake nestled inside and Dottie tucked into bed, Drew gave Grant a clap on the back. "I'll stay tonight, just to make sure things are okay. I don't have to work tomorrow."

Grant yawned and said, "That would be great. I need to get in as early as possible. We'll have a busy weekend."

Drew's two dogs were asleep in front of the fire. He cleaned up the dinner dishes and checked on Hope. He found her sleeping, still hot to the touch.

He grabbed a blanket and made for the recliner, turning on the television and lowering the volume for some company as he drifted to sleep.

Drew's beeping cell phone woke him early Saturday morning. He cracked open his eye and saw his two dogs still sleeping. The television was still on, as was the Christmas tree. He lowered the footrest and crept into the mudroom for a quick shower. He checked his mom's notes and saw the breakfast recipe for the day.

He went about gathering ingredients, and once he started his prep work, Dickens and Fletch found their way to the kitchen, noses in the air. He fed the dogs and went back to beating eggs. Grant arrived with fresh pastries.

"Wanna cup of coffee?" asked Drew.

"Nah, I've got to get back. I've got too much to do. How's Hope this morning?"

Drew shrugged as he took a sip from his cup. "Haven't checked." He gestured to the casserole dish. "I need to get this baking, and then I'll see how she is doing."

Grant waved goodbye as he hurried to the van. Drew popped the dish in the oven and tiptoed down the hallway to the Blue Room. He tapped on the door before opening it.

Hope was still asleep. He saw the glasses of water and juice were still full, as was the cup of tea. He shook his head and tapped her shoulder. "Hope, I need you to wake up and drink something."

Her eyes fluttered, and she squinted at the soft light from the lamp. She croaked and held her hand to her throat. "Your throat is worse?" he asked.

She nodded, and he handed her a glass of water. "Try to drink this. She took a sip and her brow furrowed as she swallowed.

"I think you need to see a doctor," said Drew.

She shook her head several times and mouthed a negative response. Drew pursed his lips. "I'll make you some hot tea, and then we'll see how you're doing."

She rested back against the pillows, her face flush.

He returned a few minutes later with a steaming cup and a bottle of over the counter pain relievers. He poured two of them in her hand and told her to drink the whole glass of water.

She complied and winced when she forced the capsules down. She mouthed something and made a motion like skiing. Drew nodded and said, "We'll make sure Jake goes to the parade, don't worry."

She gave him a weak smile and closed her eyes.

As soon as the commotion of breakfast was over and the guests were on their way to the festival downtown, Dottie shuffled into Hope's room. "Hope, dear, are you any better?"

Hope gave her a shrug and grabbed a pen and paper from the bedside table. She jotted a note and turned the paper to Dottie. *I'm so sorry.*

Dottie patted her shoulder. "Don't worry, my dear. We'll be fine. Drew can handle the weekend chores around here. You just rest and get better." She paused and added, "How about some food? I've got some chicken soup in the freezer."

Hope smiled and gestured with her fingers, indicating a tiny amount. Dottie and her walker clicked across the floor. "I'll be back soon." Hope nodded and sighed as she rested against the mound of pillows behind her.

Hope's eyes went wide when she saw an unfamiliar man come through her door, followed by Drew. "Hope, this is Dr. Mills. He's a friend of the family, and I called him to see if he could prescribe something. He offered to stop by and check on you."

Fear flashed across Hope's face. She shook her head. She hurried to write on her pad of paper. *No insurance. I can't afford a house call.*

Dr. Mills shook his head. "Not to worry. I owe Drew much more than this. He's been to our house dozens of times for animal emergencies. Just relax. No charge for today."

Hope tried to clear her throat and flinched with pain. Dr. Mills opened his bag and turned to Drew. "We'll be fine."

The doctor checked Hope's throat and did a thorough exam. He finished listening to her lungs and said, "As Drew suspected. I'm pretty sure you have strep throat. You also have a sinus infection. Your lungs are clear, so that's a good thing. I'll give you a course of antibiotics. You'll need to take it easy for a few days and drink lots of liquids. We can recheck you in about ten days and make sure you're well."

He asked her questions about her history, allergies, and other antibiotics she had taken and she used the notepad to answer. He jotted down notes and rummaged in his bag.

Tears leaked out of Hope's eyes. She tried to croak out her thanks but relented to the use of the notepad. *Thank you, Dr. Mills. When can I get back to work here helping Dottie?*

"You'll need at least three days on the antibiotics before you'll be able to work. If you're not feeling better by then, I need to know."

She nodded and mimed her gratitude again. He wrote her name on a bottle of pills and doled out one of them for her to take, handing her the glass of water. "If you don't rest and heal, you'll relapse, and it could be worse. Just take it easy, watch movies or something, okay?"

Hope lips turned upwards and she nodded as he bundled his things and waved goodbye. He found Drew and Dottie in the living room with the dogs and Jake. "She's going to be fine. I've started her on antibiotics and told her she needs to rest for at least three days."

Dottie smiled at Jake. "Your mommy just needs to stay in bed, and she'll be better in no time. No need to worry."

The doctor smiled at the boy. "Not at all. Just make sure you all wash your hands thoroughly. We don't need anyone else getting sick." The doctor gave them a wave as he left through the front door.

"Thanks again for the house call," said Drew, following him out to the porch. He brought in some logs from the stack outside and fed the fire.

Breakfast had been served, and the guests had dispersed while Dr. Mills had been in with Hope. Drew fixed a tray of soup and beverages and disappeared down the hall to deliver it to his patient.

He coerced Hope into sitting up and resting against the large stack of pillows so he could position the tray over her lap. She took a few sips of the rich broth and smiled. She gestured a thumbs up sign and smiled as she continued to eat.

He nodded and said, "You eat the whole bowl, and I'm going to get the breakfast dishes done. I want to see the juice and tea gone when I return, got it?"

She bobbed her head in a meek nod and continued sipping the broth.

Dottie sat with Jake and the dogs in the living room while he returned the kitchen to order and took a look at his mother's note for the breakfast plan for tomorrow. He drank another cup of coffee as he flipped through the book to get a feel for the workload in the coming days. Everyone was leaving on Monday, and they would have until Friday to get things ready again.

He tiptoed down the hallway and peeked through the doorway of the Blue Room. He saw the tray at the foot of the bed. The empty bowl, glass, and cup made him smile. Hope was fast asleep, her dark, tousled hair splayed across the pillow. He collected the tray and shut her door without making a sound.

9

Grant returned to the house with a slow cooker filled with dinner and Luna and Ginger, who joined the other three furry pooches. The guests were all out for the festival, so Dottie would be minding the house, the dogs, and keeping watch over Hope.

Dottie made sure Jake was bundled up, and his boots were snug. Hope had slept most of the day but Drew forced her to drink each time she was awake and had gotten another bowl of soup down her before it was time to leave for the parade.

The boys waved goodbye as Dottie watched from the door. Grant took the route through town so Jake could look at all the Christmas lights on Main Street. He piloted his truck up the windy road to the ski resort. Tables and chairs were set up around portable heaters and firepits near the lodge. Several portable bleachers had been added to allow for the crowd. Hundreds of festival-goers circled a giant bonfire burning well away from the lodge.

Free hot chocolate and cookies were available at locations staffed by elves with twinkling lights wrapped around them. Jake's excitement bubbled out of him in gasps and laughs. Grant had a friend save them spots at a table near a firepit with a terrific view of the mountain. They settled in and munched on treats while they waited for the parade.

Jake's eyes widened when an elf skipped over to their table and placed a candy cane and a chocolate covered marshmallow Santa in his hand. The elf gave a quick wink and was off to the next table. "Wow," Jake yelled. "This is the best Christmas ever."

Drew considered the sweets and said, "How about we take those home and wait until after dinner? You can share it with your mom."

Jake eyed the candy and then nodded his head. "Okay. We should bring her a cookie too."

Grant laughed and said, "I've got some cookies from the bakery. They're back at the house. They were leftovers from all the cookies I made for the festival tonight."

Jake gave his cookie a sheepish glance and looked up at Drew. The man smiled at Jake and said, "Go ahead, you can have one cookie. We just don't want to spoil your dinner."

As he was munching on the sugar covered cookie shaped like a snowman, the crowd began shouting and pointing up the mountain. Drew positioned Jake so he was sitting on the table looking upward. "Watch for the lights; they're just starting."

A reddish orange glow snaked down the mountain as skiers descended with their flares. It resembled a skinny line of lava oozing down the hill. It took several minutes for the first skiers to reach the lodge. As the skiers spread out, the radiant flares bounced across the dark mountain.

The crowd oohed and aahed at the luminous display and hoots of praise echoed across the vast space. Once the last skier had finished the course, brilliant fireworks shot across the dark sky. Jake shrieked with excitement as the dazzling colors lit up the mountain.

Soft thumps announced the launch of more fireworks and then the grand finale sizzled and hissed through the air. The heavens filled with starbursts and rockets of explosive colors. Jake's eyes were huge, and his mouth hung open with astonishment.

Grant pointed out his favorite displays, while Drew focused on Jake. The boy almost toppled backwards craning his neck to take in the spectacular exhibition. The pyrotechnics provided enough light to erase the winter darkness. The elves pranced from table to table, handing out marshmallows and sticks for roasting.

Drew loaded their sticks and when the last sparks of color fizzled into the once again dark sky, he handed one to Jake. The boy looked at it with questioning eyes. "Haven't you ever roasted marshmallows before?" asked Drew.

Jake shook his head. "I don't think so."

Drew and Grant showed him how it was done and soon the threesome was slipping off the golden-brown gooey messes and popping them in their mouths. When Jake took his off the stick, Drew said, "Be careful, it will be super-hot so don't burn your mouth."

Jake took a small nibble of the crunchy outer crust and then blew on the hot liquified center before shoving it into his mouth. He grinned through lips covered with the white sticky residue. "Those are so yummy."

Drew limited him to only two more, citing their waiting dinner. Jake had only one casualty of a flaming marshmallow that had to be abandoned due to its charcoal-like appearance. With a bit of practice, he mastered the art of turning it in the fire, so it came out a perfect toasted color.

They finished the last treat and traipsed to Grant's truck for the ride home. As they made their way down the mountain, Jake squealed each time he saw a decorated tree or yard. The people who lived on the mountain went all out for Christmas with most of them stringing lights in the pine trees in their yard. Some of them added extensive blow up figures, sleighs, and lights set to music.

The dogs and Dottie greeted them when they arrived. Jake was full of stories but Dottie put her fingers to her lips, "Mommy is still sleeping, so we need to be quiet."

Jake lowered his voice to a whisper and entertained Dottie with stories about the fireworks and marshmallows. While he caught her up, Grant dished up bowls of stew and cut slices of bread he brought from the bakery.

As soon as they finished dinner, Drew took Jake by the hand and said, "You're looking tired, buddy. How about pajamas and we'll get you settled in your fort with Scout?"

The boy gave a slow nod coupled with a long yawn. Dottie and Grant watched as Drew hoisted Jake out of his chair. The boy wrapped his arms around Drew's neck and rested his head on his broad shoulders.

When the two had left, Dottie leaned to Grant and whispered, "He sure has taken a liking to Jake."

Grant nodded. "I'm sure he reminds Drew of Danny. He's around the same age as Danny was when he died."

Tears formed in Dottie's eyes. "It's wonderful to have a child around the house."

Grant rose and gave his mom a long hug. "How about I help you to your room and then I'll get the kitchen cleaned up and ready for tomorrow?"

She rested her head on his shoulder and said, "Thank you. I appreciate all you and your brother are doing to help around here."

Drew slept in his old room and rolled out of bed early Sunday morning. After fussing in the kitchen and making sure the fire was roaring, he tapped on Hope's door. He heard nothing. With great care, he turned the knob and stepped inside. The soft light from the lamp illuminated her sleeping form.

He made his way to her and touched her forehead with his hand. The fever was gone. He turned to leave when he heard a whisper. "Jake?"

"No, Hope. It's Drew. It's early. I was just checking on you. I think your fever is gone. Jake's still asleep."

Her eyes fluttered, and she bobbed her head in understanding.

"I'll be back with some breakfast later. You rest." He took slow steps out the door and closed it with a soft click. He got back to his morning duties and readied the kitchen for the first meal of the day.

The guests chattered during breakfast, praising the fireworks and torchlight parade. They had enjoyed themselves until late in the evening and raved about the festival activities and the wonderful town of Silver Falls. They lingered longer than Drew had hoped, drinking cup after cup of coffee.

Grant arrived and offered to take the dogs and Jake for a walk to give them all a bit of exercise. He mentioned the idea of the free Christmas movie at the theatre later in the morning. Jake grinned and ran through the house with gusto.

Dottie stayed at the table and visited with the guests, reminiscing about the festivals of bygone years. Drew clanged a few dishes around in the kitchen, hoping they'd take the hint. After he had everything cleaned, he moved to the large table and said, "So, you folks are all checking out today. I've got your receipts ready, and we'd be happy to help you with your luggage."

The group began shifting out of their chairs and made

their way to their rooms. Within the hour, they had left the guest house and Drew was busy making a tray of food for Hope. He added a cup of tea to the tray and toted it down the hallway.

He found Hope sitting upright in bed with her tablet. With a quick movement, she flipped the cover and set the tablet to the side. Drew placed the tray in front of her and said, "You're looking a bit better today."

She shrugged and gestured with her finger and thumb to indicate she felt a bit better. As he moved his hand away, he displaced the tablet. It fell to the floor, the cover opening.

The screen came to life, and he saw a photo of what looked like a graduation, with Hope, a man with his arm around her, Jake, and a young woman decked out in a cap and gown. The young woman had beautiful, long, dark hair and eyes that mirrored Hope's. "Sorry," he said, picking it up for her.

"Is that your family?" he asked, handing her the tablet.

Panic flashed in her tired eyes. She looked at the tablet and then to Drew. Tears leaked down her cheeks, and she gave him a resigned nod.

"I've upset you. I'm sorry." He pulled a chair from the corner closer to the bed. "You don't have to tell me, but I'm willing to listen." She looked at him and remained silent. "Or you can say nothing at all. I just want to make sure you're okay."

He gestured to the tray. "You need to eat before it's cold. Scrambled eggs, orange juice, tea, and toast, if you can handle it."

She sniffed, and he passed her a box of tissues. She dabbed at her eyes and picked up her fork. While she ate he regaled her with stories from the festival last night and told her about Jake roasting marshmallows.

Her eyes lit up with happiness when he described their

adventure. "You should have seen him watching the sky. He had a look of pure wonder on his face."

Hope clutched the mug of tea in her hands and whispered, "Thank you. It means the world to me that he had fun."

"Grant took him downtown to the Christmas movie this morning. I'm sure he'll treat him to lunch while they're there."

Hope smiled and continued to eat while Drew rambled on about the activities and told her about the guests who had left. She finished her meal and rested against the pillows behind her.

"I'll take this out of the way. I'm going to get started on cleaning the rooms, and you should take a nap."

She whispered, "Leave it all, and I'll do it tomorrow. Doc said I should be better by then."

"I've got today off, so I'll do all I can, and you can finish up the loose ends when you're feeling well. Don't get in a hurry. We have until Friday to get things shipshape."

He returned the tray to the kitchen and fetched her a fresh glass of water. When he returned to her room, she was fast asleep.

When Grant and Jake returned in the late afternoon, they found all the dogs napping with Dottie in her family room. Footfalls from upstairs signaled Drew was working on the guest rooms.

Grant got started on dinner and Jake stationed himself at the island to watch and chat while Grant worked. He was making his mother's chicken, and he had finished peeling the last potato when Drew appeared.

"How was the movie?"

Eager to share his day, Jake provided a narration of the movie, treats consumed, and lunch at the Burger Barn. Grant chuckled listening to the enthusiastic account of the day.

"I talked to your mom this morning, and she's feeling better." Jake gave a toothy grin at the good news. "We still need to let her rest and keep you away from those nasty germs, but I told her all about the fireworks last night, and she was so excited for you."

While dinner baked in the oven, Drew commandeered Jake to help finish some of the laundry upstairs. By the time they were done, Dottie was in the kitchen helping with the salad, the dogs had been fed, and Grant was getting the meal out of the oven.

Drew made a tray for Hope and told Jake he could follow him but had to stay in the hallway and wave to his mom from the doorway. Jake hurried down the hall, his socks sliding on the wooden floor.

When Drew opened the door, Jake yelled, "Mommy, Mommy."

She waved and mouthed, "Hi, buddy."

Drew delivered the dinner tray and noticed her hair was wet. "Did you take a shower?"

She nodded. "I needed one and feel better, but now I'm tired," she whispered. "I'm on the mend. I can tell."

"We'll leave you to your dinner. Hopefully, tomorrow you'll be up and about and feeling better."

Jake waved and said, "Goodnight, Mommy. I saved you a treat for when you are feeling better."

Monday morning, Hope was up early. She sipped a cup of tea dosed with honey. The house was quiet. Jake was sleeping in the boys' old room, and Drew had gone home last night, confident his mom could manage without any guests.

The sky was beginning to bloom with the first wisps of soft light. Hope snuggled into the blanket and let the slow flicker of flames in the fireplace soothe her. She opened her tablet and scrolled through the latest news.

As she read the headlines, her thoughts drifted to her situation with the car. Without guests until the weekend, she could put in extra hours at the bakery, but couldn't risk wearing herself out and relapsing.

She ran through the numbers, as she had done countless times. It was going to take months of work. Dottie wouldn't need help for that long, and she didn't want to take advantage of her generosity.

She heard the back door open and the soft shuffle of footsteps. She knew it was Grant, delivering fresh pastries. He didn't linger, and she didn't move from her place on the couch. She heard the door close again and went back to musing.

She felt a tap on her shoulder and opened her eyes in surprise. The sun had risen, and Drew loomed over her. "How are you feeling?" he asked.

"Better, thanks," she said, her voice weak, but audible.

"I came by early on my way to work. Mom and Jake are still asleep. I rearranged my appointments in case I was needed here this morning." He retreated to fill a cup with coffee and rejoined her in the living room.

He took note of the tablet. "Have you been reading?"

She shrugged. "No, just skimming the news and trying to figure out how to accelerate my earnings so I can get my stupid car fixed."

He nodded as he took another sip from his cup. "You should probably worry about recovering from strep throat before you get too far ahead of yourself. Are you in a hurry to leave?"

"No, not really. I just feel bad and don't want to take advantage of your mom. Or any of you."

"She's not going to be going up those stairs for a couple of months. I'm not sure she has come to terms with it. Until I filled in this weekend, I didn't realize how much work there is around here." He cleared his throat. "She'd, uh, we'd all be grateful if you could stay and handle the place until she's capable. I also think it's worth much more than a room here. Let us pay you something to compensate for your work."

She held the warm cup in her hands and gazed at the fire. "I wouldn't feel right. On days when there are no guests, there's not much I need to do. I don't think your mom can afford to pay me if there's no income."

"How about we agree to a small payment only on days we have guests? The other days you can make sure Mom gets meals and take care of the normal chores, but we need to compensate you for the extra work. It's too much."

Hope contemplated the offer. "That sounds reasonable. Just pay Chet down at the garage. He can put it on my bill. I'll commit to stay until Dottie doesn't need the help, but I don't want to be a burden."

Drew chuckled. "Trust me, you're not a burden. If we didn't have your help, we'd have to hire a full-time caregiver and someone to do all the other chores. You're a bargain." He finished his coffee. "Not to mention Mom thinks the world of you and Jake."

"She's a sweetheart and Jake adores her."

"It's been a long time since Mom's had a child around the house. Well, since, Danny, of course. Danny would be twenty now." Drew's voice was thick with emotion. "Not a day goes by when I don't think of him. And Laura. A part of me was lost that night. Forever."

"I'm not sure how you survive such a loss." A tear leaked out of Hope's eye.

The sound of Scout thundering down the hall and the squeals from Jake interrupted their conversation. "Mommy, Mommy," said the boy as he jumped onto the couch.

She stroked Jake's head and squeezed him tight. "I've missed you, buddy."

10

At Dottie's insistence, Hope lounged most of the day. The only thing she accomplished was changing the bedding in the Blue Room and disinfecting everything. They ate pastries for breakfast, watched television, took naps, and listened to Jake read stories. The doctor called to check on Hope and urged her to continue to rest and limit her activity.

The dinner hour rolled around, and Grant arrived with Chinese takeout. Drew came through the door as they were eating. "Sorry, long day." He helped himself to a plate.

Dottie finished and said, "I'm tired. I think I'm going to call it a night." Grant helped her up and offered to see her to her room.

"Can I sleep in their room again?" asked Jake.

Hope raised her brows, and Dottie answered, "Of course you can. Come on, and we'll get you settled."

Jake wrapped his arms around Hope's neck. "I know you'll miss me, but I like having my own room again. It has two beds." He giggled and followed Dottie.

Hope shook her head and smiled. "He's something else."

She collected her plate and the others and took them to the sink.

Grant breezed through the kitchen and said, "Night all. I've got to get going."

"I plan to be in tomorrow to help. I'm so sorry I've let you down these last few days," she said, finishing loading the dishwasher.

"Not to worry. If you're up to it, I'll see you tomorrow. This weekend is the huge cookie exchange, so we'll be slammed all week." He turned and waved at Drew. "See ya."

"Jake will want to go to the cookie exchange this weekend. It started decades ago and involved a community cookie exchange where everyone brought a tray of their favorite cookies. It's grown to a huge event. We block off Main Street, and the whole place is filled with cookies and Christmas treats."

"I take it more people order their cookie trays these days?"

Drew nodded. "Grant gets a ton of orders from customers. Not to mention the City of Silver Falls, local businesses, and several organizations. They all have booths or tables during the event. Lots of money raised for charity with donations and raffles."

"Sounds fun. Jake will be all over anything related to cookies." She fixed herself a cup of tea and moved to the chair closest to the fireplace.

Drew sighed as he took a seat on the sofa and eased his feet out of his shoes. "It was definitely a Monday." He went on to tell her about his day, including two calls to ranches out of town.

"So, what did you do before you set out on your adventure across America?" he asked.

She kept the cup at her lips. "Not much. I haven't worked since college."

"Tell me about your family. The one in the photo on your tablet." He pointed to the red case on the table beside her chair.

She sucked in a breath. She opened the tablet and scrolled to the photo he had seen. "She's my daughter, Tina. She's in college now. Tina's the same age as your Danny."

"And the man is your husband?"

Her lips tightened, and her mouth disappeared. She bobbed her head. "It's a long story."

Drew moved his legs on to the couch and sprawled across it, raising his coffee cup, "We've got all night."

"One of Tina's first assignments in her science class this semester had to do with genetics. They were studying blood types, and the assignment was to gather the types of her parents and siblings."

"I wasn't aware of the entire project, she just called me and said she was studying and needed to know my blood type. I didn't think much of it, until a few days later."

"Brian, my husband, stormed into the house after work one night. He was out of control. He demanded to know who Tina's real father was and who I had been having an affair with." She grabbed a tissue and dabbed at her eyes.

"I should have started at the beginning of the story. She stuck her finger deep into the inside cover of her tablet. She teased something forward and unearthed an old photograph.

She smiled when she looked at it and walked over so Drew could see it. "This is Henry with me. We met in college."

Drew took in the photo of a young smiling Hope and a dark haired young main gazing at her. They were in front of a huge tree, standing on the grass. "You were very young."

"Yes. It seems like an entire lifetime ago. We were engaged to be married. We wanted to wait until we both finished graduate school. He was kind. Intelligent. Full of life. It was all so perfect."

"So, what happened?" he asked, his brow wrinkled.

"We had plans to visit his family. They summered on Mackinac Island. I had a few things to do so Henry went on without me, and I was going to meet them all in a couple of days. There was freak storm, and Henry's plane went down. He died." Her voice cracked and tears streamed down her face.

"I found out I was pregnant two weeks later."

"I'm so sorry, Hope. I'm sure you were devastated."

She took a moment to compose herself. "I don't have to tell you what it's like to lose someone you love. I didn't know what to do." She went on to explain she had met Brian soon after Henry's death. Her degree was in art history, and she worked at a gallery and Brian attended one of their galas.

"I was stupid and vulnerable. I saw a way out of my situation and took it. It was a decision I've come to regret."

Drew listened without interruption as she bared her soul, hanging her head in shame when she told him Brian proposed marriage when she told him she was pregnant. "With the gift of hindsight, I should have just powered through on my own." She paused and added, "But, I would have never had my son."

She explained that Brian was a financial manager. He provided a life full of material possessions, money, vacations, and a lifestyle most would envy. "He's always been dominant and controlling, but I lacked for nothing, so never questioned much."

"I take it Tina revealed the results of her genetic study and informed him there was no way he could be her father?"

Hope's head sagged into her shoulders. "Exactly. We both have type O blood. Tina has type B. It's impossible."

"Her father would have to have type B or AB," added Drew.

She tipped her head. "You would know, with your medical background." She took a sip of tea. "That's the day my world changed."

Over the next hours, she described the events leading up to her decision to leave her home. "Brian was in a rage, and it escalated to him insinuating our son wasn't his. He made Tina analyze his blood type against ours. She explained the blood type information could only eliminate someone from being a parent. It couldn't provide definite paternity. He ordered a DNA test."

She wiped at her eyes again. "I told him the whole story about Henry and apologized for not telling him about the pregnancy. He didn't want to hear it. Neither did Tina." She took in a deep breath and glanced out the window before continuing. "The last straw was when he threatened me in front of my son." She put her hand to her throat and rubbed it. "He hurt me and said awful things about me. He told me to get out and take my son with me."

"That's when you decided to leave?"

She nodded. "I got in touch with an old college roommate Brian had never met and asked her to help me get a vehicle. I sold all my jewelry and clothes and took some money I had saved over the years. My mother always told me to have a separate savings account just for me, and I'm thankful for her advice."

"Jake was scared and questioned everything, so I just told him we were going on an adventure. I told the school I was homeschooling and ordered the materials and we took off one morning after Brian went to work."

"Has he been looking for you?"

She shrugged her shoulders. "I don't know. I left my cell phone. The car is in my old roommate's cousin's name. I'm not using credit cards. I've tried to disappear. Hope and Jake aren't even our real names. Brian scared me and told me he wanted me gone."

"What about the police?"

Fresh tears trickled down her face. "I should have called them myself when he hurt me. I was too afraid they wouldn't believe me because I lied about my pregnancy." She took a breath and added, "Brian has powerful friends. He's connected. I would never win." She shuddered. "I don't think he would involve the police because of what he did to me in front of Jake. I'm more concerned he'll use private sources to find me."

"I understand you wanting to be careful. You're safe here. Just relax and rest. You don't have anything to worry about in Silver Falls. I'm sorry for what you're going through." He paused and added, "To be honest, I was suspicious of you and your story. I'm sorry I didn't trust you, and with what you've said, I understand why you're doing what you're doing."

"I had to protect my son from all of that. I've lost my daughter in the process, but he's too young to understand all of this. I want to keep him safe and keep his childhood intact."

"I understand protecting those you love. If I could have saved Danny and Laura, I would have done anything." Drew glanced at his watch and stood. "It's almost time to get up. I need to get going. Are you going to be okay?"

She nodded. "Please don't say anything to anyone."

He gripped her shoulder, and she tensed. "I won't say a word. I promise. I'll talk to you later. Call my cell if you or Mom need anything."

After Drew left, Hope went back to her room, stunned that it was time to get ready for the day. After a long bout of crying in the shower, she composed herself and got dressed.

When she emerged, she found Jake and Scout in the living room, reading a book.

She made sure Dottie didn't need anything, offered to pick up her marketing, and set off for the bakery. She ended up working all day. In addition to his regular baking, Grant had the daunting task of delivering over three thousand cookies by the weekend. Hope promised to work each day, to help.

Hope shuffled into the house Thursday night, exhausted from the last three days of nonstop prepping and cleaning at the bakery. Drew had taken over dinner duties for the week and there was a plate waiting for her in the oven.

As she was taking her plate to the counter, Drew came around the corner. "Hey," he whispered. "Mom and Jake are asleep."

"Thanks for stepping in with him for me this week. I can't believe the workload at Grant's. I have a new appreciation for Christmas cookies." She dug into the chicken casserole. "This tastes so good."

"I was hoping to catch you tonight. I, uh, well, I did a little research online. I don't want to alarm you. I'm trying to help. I'm pretty sure you're Abby Pearson, and your husband is Brian Pearson."

The color drained from her face. "How do you know that?"

11

Drew held up his hands. "I didn't tell anyone, so don't get excited. I'm the only one who knows." He fixed a cup of coffee and made her a tea, talking as he filled the cups. "I searched a few newspapers and used social media. Your daughter's profile gave me more information, and then I pieced it together. Found a newspaper photo of you and Brian at some bigwig event, and it listed your name."

"Why, though?" She shoved her half-eaten meal to the middle of the island.

"I wanted to see if I could figure out a solution to your problem. I have a friend, who is a lawyer. He used to practice in Chicago. I sent him an email."

"You what? Are you crazy?" Hope's voice bordered on hysteria.

"Wait, wait a minute." He put his hand on top of hers. "I didn't tell him your name, nothing. I told him I had a touchy situation and wanted to get his advice."

"He might know Brian or his partners. I've got to leave now." Tears sprang into her eyes, and she stood. "I can't leave. I don't have a car." She began to pace.

"I'm not doing a good job of explaining things. Just wait a minute. Take a breath and listen to everything. Can you do that?" He gestured to her chair. "Please?"

Defiance flashed in her eyes. She marched over to the counter and with a stern glare, plunked into the chair. "Only because I don't have an option."

"So, my buddy, Mark, is a stand-up guy. He doesn't know your name or Brian's. I explained that I have a friend in your situation. I told him about the threats and physical altercation. Told him you have a seven-year-old son and your fears."

She stared at him, shaking her head with disgust. "I trusted you, Drew. I really did."

"You still can. Just let me finish. You said you have pictures of the altercation with Brian where he hurt you?"

She nodded. "Good," he said. "Mark said he could use those facts to keep your location a secret. He's willing to represent you for free. He's confident Brian, like most bullies, will fold when he's hit with some legal action. He's sure he can get you custody and a divorce and most likely some alimony."

"His advice is to file here in Nevada. He works in Reno and can handle it all. You have to live here for six weeks to file. The good news is, we can count all the time you've been here. That means it could be filed by Christmas."

She frowned. "Aren't we in California?"

"We're only about five miles from California. The shortcut you took put you in our state."

She let out a long sigh. "I don't know what to do. What if Brian finds us?"

"He won't. Let Mark do some digging. He knows how guys like Brian operate. He won't jeopardize you or Jake. By the way, what is Jake's real name?"

"Tyler. Just don't confuse him. I told him we were on an adventure and playing pretend. He's embraced it now, so I don't want to get him any more screwed up than I already have."

"Do you want a divorce?"

"I haven't given it much thought. I couldn't figure out how to do it without it turning into a huge battle. I suppose I do. I don't want to go back to Brian. I don't feel safe. I don't want Jake around him. It's a huge mess." She bent and put her head down on the counter atop her arms.

"Okay, I understand. Like I said, Mark doesn't know you or your name. He's not going to take any action. I just wanted to get some legal advice. That way you know your options. I don't think you can just keep running forever."

She turned her head to the side. "I'm just too tired right now to think. I'm scared and worried and don't know what to do. I've got to get some sleep. Tomorrow's a full day."

Drew stood and pushed his chair to the counter. "I'm sorry, Hope. I didn't mean to make things worse." He called for Dickens and Fletch. The dogs scampered from the living room and followed him to the door.

Hope hadn't slept well and yawned as she made coffee Friday morning. Knowing, she'd have a long day, she put together the ingredients for her favorite soup in the slow cooker. She had tossed and turned all night, thinking about what Drew had said last night. With all the rooms ready and things organized for the arrivals this afternoon, she set out for the bakery as soon as Jake and Dottie finished their breakfast.

The bakery was buzzing with activity. Customers stopped by throughout the day to pick up their orders. Grant asked Hope to accompany him in the bakery van to deliver the larger orders. As they chatted and worked, Hope kept watching for a sign that Grant might know what she had told Drew, but there wasn't an inkling.

They spent several hours toting boxes into businesses, lingering at each while Grant visited. Everyone knew Grant, and they were quick to dispense holiday wishes as they complimented his cookies.

They grabbed sandwiches for lunch in between stops. Children and adults alike, strolled through the streets of town, taking in the decorations and chatting about the upcoming cookie exchange. Immersed in their idyllic surroundings, Hope said, "Makes me wish I could stay here forever."

Grant nodded as he swallowed a bite. "Silver Falls is a wonderful place to live, especially for a kid. It's small and safe. Everybody knows everybody." He winked and added, "Which is nice, but can be a pain."

"I think it's nice. It's like having an extended family looking out for you."

He nodded. "It's all I've ever known. I love it here. Drew and I both want to be here for Mom. It's home."

They finished lunch and hopped in the van to deliver the rest of the cookies. With only a few boxes left, he offered to drop her back at the guest house before three o'clock, so she'd be ready for guests. He pulled into the driveway and handed her a box of cookies to go with the bread she had selected for dinner. "These are for the guests and all of us. Thanks for your help today."

She smiled and said, "Jake will be out of his mind when he sees these. See you at dinner tonight."

She opened the door, and the aroma of chicken soup wafted through the air. She was able to sneak the bakery box into the kitchen. After putting a festive selection of cookies on a plate by the coffee station, she hid the box under a towel. Jake didn't need to start any earlier than necessary.

She found Jake and Dottie in her living area, both fast asleep. She tiptoed back down the hall and made herself a cup of tea. The idea of divorcing Brian and the risk of him finding them dominated her thoughts. It wasn't long before the front door chimed and the first guests arrived.

Hope welcomed them, showed them to their rooms, and invited them to enjoy a beverage and cookie. Dottie and Jake had woken from their nap and stationed themselves in the kitchen, where they nibbled on cookies and visited with the newcomers.

They didn't linger long, as they were excited to see the festival and get their weekend started. Dottie shared her restaurant recommendations and made sure they knew about all early cookie stops that would be open tonight. Drew and his dogs came through the back door, as the last couple set out for downtown Silver Falls.

"Something smells good," he said, sniffing the air.

"Hope made soup for us," said Dottie.

"And Grant sent us some cookies." Jake hopped from his chair to point at the almost empty plate next to the coffee.

Drew followed Jake's suggestion and nabbed two cookies from the plate. "Yum," he said, taking a bite. "I'm starving. It's been a long day."

The crunch of tires announced the arrival of Grant and his two dogs. They clambered into the kitchen, and all five dogs scrambled to follow Drew to their feeding bowls. With one cookie in his mouth and the other in his hand, he attempted to scoop out their servings.

Jake offered to help and marveled at Drew as he chomped the cookie without using his hands. "How do you do that?"

"Many years of practice." He popped the other one into his mouth and scooped while Jake held the bowls for him.

"That's so cool. Can you teach me?"

Drew glanced into the kitchen and put his finger to his lips. "I don't think your mom or my mom would approve."

Jake wrinkled his nose and pouted his lips. "Yeah, Mom doesn't like me to eat like an animal."

Drew stifled a chuckle as they finished the chore and left the dogs to their dinner. Back in the kitchen, Hope was ladling soup into deep ceramic bowls, embellished with snowmen. The bread was sliced, and on the table, along with a salad.

Drew and Jake washed their hands in the sink in the mudroom before they joined the others at the table. Grant passed along greetings from his cookie customers. They all knew Dottie was out of commission and wished her their best. "I miss all the excitement of the season," she said, with sadness in her eyes.

"We're going to the cookie exchange tomorrow. Maybe you can come with us?" said Jake.

Dottie smiled and said, "We'll see how I feel tomorrow. It's so crowded downtown, I'm not sure it's a good idea."

Grant winked and said, "I could block off the bench in front of the bakery and reserve it for you. If you get cold, you could hang out inside."

"I'll bring you home if you get tired, Mom," added Drew.

Dottie dabbed at her eyes with the corner of her napkin. "You are the best sons in the world. That sounds like fun." She finished her soup and said, "And, tomorrow night we're having pizza to celebrate. My treat."

Jake eyes went wild, and he trembled with excitement. "I love pizza," he said in a monster-like voice.

"Cool it," said Hope, admonishment in her eyes. "Finish your dinner and then it's time for a bath. You have a big day tomorrow."

He hurried and scooped the soup into his mouth, nodding and yammering to himself.

"I think he's had too many cookies today," said Hope, rolling her eyes. "Just think he'll get even more sugar tomorrow at the festival."

Drew offered to clean up the dinner dishes while Hope led Jake to the bath and bed. When she returned, she found only Drew in the living room with the three dogs. "Where is everyone?" she asked, walking past to get a cup of tea.

"Grant was beat and has a long day tomorrow. Mom wanted to get to bed early so she can go to the festival with us."

"She's getting cabin fever stuck in here all the time. I'm sure she's frustrated."

He nodded. "It'll be good for her to get out tomorrow, even if it's just for an hour or two." He left the chair and returned with the plate of cookies and placed it on the table between them.

He bit the head off of a snowman and said, "Did you give any more thought to my offer?"

"It's all I've been thinking about. I couldn't sleep last night. I'm torn."

"I promise you, you'll be safe here. Brian will never know you're here. Mark understands the situation and assures me he can keep your whereabouts secret. You'll just have to go to Reno when it's time to sign documents."

She stared at her cup. "You said he could just start investigating and learn more, right?"

He nodded. "That's right. He won't file anything or alert him. Just check things out and get a better idea of what he can do for you."

Lost in thought, she gazed at the Christmas tree, while Drew continued. "I know you're trying to protect Jake and I realize you're scared. You're going to want him to be able to have a normal life and stop your pretend game. You'll want him to be able to go to school again and have friends who know his name."

A tear leaked from her eye. He reached across to wipe it from her cheek. "I'm sorry, Hope. I just want you and Jake secure and happy. You, and Jake deserve to have your life back."

She took a deep breath and said, "Okay, have him start the investigation only. Once I know more, I'll make a decision." She paused and said, "I don't care about never seeing Brian again, but Tina." Silent tears sprinkled her cheeks. "I don't want this to be the end."

"I understand. I don't really see a way to Tina as long as Brian is still in the picture. There's no safe way for you to reach out to her."

"I know. It's a mess of a situation. I've been thinking about it ever since I left home and still have no solution."

"I'll call Mark in the morning and get him started." He finished his tea and stood, squeezing her shoulder in a firm grip. "You're making the right decision."

She heard him and the dogs leave. She continued to sit, as if hypnotized by the Christmas tree. "I hope Drew's right, and I'm not making a huge mistake," she whispered.

12

The guests devoured the pecan maple French toast casserole Hope had prepared for Saturday morning. Drew arrived as the guests were finishing their coffee and making noises about leaving for the day.

He loaded up on a huge square of the casserole, added several pieces of bacon, and some fruit to his plate, and joined Jake at the table. "How's it going, big guy?"

Jake smiled with a milk mustache and said, "Good. I'm ready to go to town."

Hope collected the dirty plates and said, "It'll be a little while, Jake. I've got to get the rooms freshened upstairs before we leave."

"How about you go check on Mom, and I'll come and get you when I'm done? I need your help walking the dogs this morning." Drew wiggled his brows at the boy.

Jake slid out of his seat and raced across the kitchen. Drew lowered his voice and said, "I talked to Mark this morning. He sent a sheet for you to fill out and wants you to forward the photos you kept. You can send them to me, and I'll get them to him, so there's no direct contact with you." He finished his meal and plucked a piece of folded paper from his jacket pocket on the way to the sink.

Hope nodded as she finished loading the dishwasher. "Okay, I'll do it today."

"I'll go rescue Mom and get Jake and the dogs out of your hair."

Hope finished the rooms and had time for a cup of tea with Dottie while they waited for Drew to return. Dottie was wearing a bit of makeup and her favorite Christmas sweater in honor of the day's festivities.

They heard the back door open, and Jake came running into the living room. "Are you ready, Mom?" His smile full and his cheeks rosy.

"We're ready. Let's go," she said, jumping from her chair.

Drew loaded his mom and her walker into the SUV, while Hope and Jake got into the backseat. He slipped into a parking spot behind the bakery. He helped his mother navigate the alley and get to the bench Grant had reserved.

The sidewalks were filled with townspeople, busy visiting the shops and stores, collecting cookies. Dottie made sure Jake had a sturdy container with a lid from her stash in the kitchen. He gave her a quick hug and promised to bring her some cookies, as he tugged on Hope's jacket, urging her to follow him.

Carolers dressed in Victorian costumes circled through the crowd singing the classics. Jake rushed to each shop and began filling his container. Everyone Hope passed greeted her with warm Christmas wishes and a smile. She made Jake slow down at a gift shop. A snow globe caught her eye, and she went to the shelf for a closer look.

Inside was a tiny replica of Silver Falls. She recognized

the giant tree on Main Street and the decorated shops along the street, all with tiny lights that were illuminated. Mesmerized, she watched as glittery snow fell all around the perfect town. Nostalgia tugged at her heart, as she listened to the melody of songs she remembered from her childhood. She grimaced when she saw the price tag.

Jake was busy adding to his cookie collection, and charming the clerks in the shop. One of them approached, as Hope turned away from the collection of snow globes. "Those are one of our bestsellers. Aren't they lovely?" she asked.

"They're beautiful. Not in my budget at the moment, I'm afraid."

The cheerful woman lowered her voice and said, "They go on sale the day after Christmas, so check back with us."

Hope thanked her and steered Jake out of the store. By the time they set out for their return trip to the bakery, Jake's container was crammed with treats. Hope carried a bag that one of the shops had given him, and it was bursting with cookies too. He skipped ahead of her, delighted with his bounty.

"Now, Jake, you are only allowed three cookies each day. We can put them in the freezer and save them, but you can't just gobble them down. You'll get sick."

"I have to give some of them to Dottie. I promised. I need to share them with Drew, too. Grant already has all the cookies at the bakery, so he doesn't need any more."

His kindness warmed her heart. "That's very nice of you to share. We'll put the leftovers in a special spot in the freezer, and then you can pick out what you want each day."

He turned and rushed to her, putting his arms around her. "I love you, Mommy. I love Christmas here."

It was mid-afternoon when they returned, and Dottie was no longer on the bench outside the bakery. Hope ushered

Jake through the door and checked the faces at the tables. No Drew. No Dottie. She held Jake's hand, and they made their way to the side counter, where Grant was boxing pastries.

He looked up and said, "Hey, guys. How was the cookie run?"

With a huge grin, Jake held up his stash. "Quite lucrative," Hope said with a laugh.

"Drew took Mom home but said to tell you to wait. He'll be right back. He's got a surprise for you two." As he taped the box shut, he winked. He handed it off to one of his staff and said, "How about a couple of hot chocolates while you wait?"

Not waiting for an answer, he made two cups and set them in front of Hope. "We'll sit in the corner and wait for Drew. Would you mind holding these?" She handed him the containers of cookies.

"Sure thing. I'll keep them safe."

They were still sipping their cocoa when Drew returned. "Is your mom okay?" asked Hope.

He nodded. "She's fine. Just worn out from all the visiting and activity. She hasn't been upright for that many hours since she took her fall. She's going to take a nap, so she's ready for pizza tonight."

"Grant said you had a surprise for us." Jake's eyes sparkled with curiosity.

Drew checked his watch. "That I do. Let's take a walk, and I'll show you." He led the way through the crowded bakery and into the crisp air.

He guided them away from the activity and across a few blocks. The glow of colored lights on the gazebo beckoned them to the park. Horses circled the white structure in the middle of the park. Two beautiful steeds stood hooked to a red sleigh, waiting. Festive red ribbons and bells outfitted the shiny chestnut horses.

Jake began to run when they hit the edge of the park. They hurried to keep up with him. Drew shook hands with the man standing near the horses. After chatting for a few moments, Drew turned his attention to the horses. He spoke to them while he scratched them behind the ears. Each of them nudged him with their noses.

The driver approached the sleigh and said, "Hop on in there, young man."

Drew lifted Jake and stepped inside. He placed the boy in the middle of the red velvet seat and turned to offer Hope his hand. She snuggled on one side of Jake and Drew took the other. The driver gave them a soft red blanket trimmed in a white furry material.

As Hope tucked the heavy blanket around Jake, he whispered, "This is the best day ever."

The driver took his seat in front of them and prodded the horses to move. As the horses trotted along the cobblestone pathway, the clip-clop of their hooves and the jingle of their bells provided a relaxing rhythm. They followed a circuitous route as the driver meandered through the residential blocks with the most decorated homes.

Jake kept gasping as he pointed out his favorites, which changed each time he saw a new house. Dusk was settling over Silver Falls, and the view as they approached Main Street was breathtaking. The snowy mountain dotted with trees loomed above the picturesque town, decked out in holiday splendor.

Fat lazy flakes of snow began to fall, as the horses traveled down the street at a slow pace. Passersby waved and greeted them. Hope heard many of them call out "Hey, Doc," as they made their way down the street. When they neared the giant tree in the middle of the street, the driver paused. Hope dug for her phone and took several photos. With the extra height of the sleigh, she captured the colorful tree against the backdrop of the mountain without any people.

"It looks just like that snow globe you liked in the store today, Mommy."

Hope nodded as she finished taking the pictures. "It does. It's perfect."

Drew asked the driver to stop again when they went past the tree and offered to take Hope and Drew's photo with the tree behind them. She handed him her phone, and he captured several of the two of them. When he sat down, Jake said, "Take one of all of us now."

Drew obliged and took some with his phone and Hope's, Jake grinning from ear to ear in all of them. The driver turned at the end of the street and took them around the corner to Silver Falls City Hall. Garland and lights were draped over the entrance. Thousands of lights decorated the bushes and trees surrounding the building and in the small square behind it where a fountain spouted.

"Wow, it's beautiful," said Hope. She took several more photos before the driver urged the horses down the road.

"It's getting cold," said Hope, snuggling closer to her son and pulling the blanket up to her chin.

Drew inched closer to Jake and reached his arm around the back of both of them, holding onto Hope's shoulder. "We'll be back soon. I don't want you getting sick again."

Hope rested her head against his arm, happier than she had felt in a long time. The snow was getting heavier. Jake squealed with excitement when Drew mentioned building a snowman tomorrow.

Hope shut her eyes and listened to the cadence of the horses' hooves, the tinkle of the bells, and the fervor of her son's chatter about snowmen, dogs, cookies, and pizza. As she listened, she realized Drew was just as excited as Jake. She hadn't been this happy in a long time.

When they arrived with the pizzas, Grant was already home. He and Dottie were in the living room visiting, while the dogs rested in front of the fire. "We were getting worried about you with all this snow," said Dottie.

"Not to worry. The pizza place was jammed tonight. Everybody in town had the same idea, I guess." He carried the boxes to the kitchen.

Hope collected their boots and coats and put them in the mud room, before getting plates and napkins organized. As Jake was about to stuff another piece of pizza into his mouth, he drew a sharp breath. "My cookies," he yelled.

Grant chuckled and held up his hands. "Don't worry. I brought them home." He pointed at the kitchen. "They're on the counter by the sink."

At the relief of a near catastrophe, Jake let out a long breath. "Oh, thank goodness. I just remembered them."

The adults laughed at the boy's intense reaction. Drew turned to him and said, "Tell Dottie about our visit to the park."

With dramatic facial expressions and even a reenactment of the horses trotting, he gave her a detailed description of their sleigh ride. He was on the edge of hysteria when Hope dragged him to the bedroom to get his pajamas.

He was asleep in her bed before she closed the door. She joined the others in the kitchen. "Well, he dropped like a heavy rock in the lake. I think he wore himself out today."

While Drew did the dishes, she put together the egg bake for tomorrow's breakfast. Grant wished them a good night and left, promising to visit Sunday afternoon and bring dinner.

Dottie watched as Hope followed her recipe. "Your breakfast this morning was wonderful, Hope. You're doing such a fine job. I can't imagine what I would do without you."

Hope wrapped the baking dish in foil and stuck it in the fridge. "I'm the one who couldn't survive without you." She glanced at Drew. "All of you. I don't know what we would have done without your generosity."

Dottie strained to get up from the chair. "I'm a firm believer in all things happening for a reason. People come into our lives for a purpose." She set off with her walker. "I'm tired and heading to bed. Good night you two."

Drew offered to help her, but she waved him back into the kitchen. "I'll shout if I need help."

As she finished the dishes from her breakfast prep, Hope wished Dottie a good night. She spied Jake's cookies and separated them into smaller groups for the freezer. As she packaged them, she popped a snowball cookie between her teeth.

Drew walked by and saw it hanging out of her mouth. "Jake told me you don't like him to eat cookies like an animal."

She hadn't seen him and startled at his voice. She shoved the powdered sugar ball into her mouth. "Cookie? What cookie?" Her voice muffled, she began to laugh.

Drew brushed his fingers over her lips. He showed her the white dust on the tips. "Evidence, my friend."

She laughed and said, "Can you be bribed not to tell him?"

He wiggled his eyebrows at her. "Depends. What's the offer?"

She shrugged. "A cookie?"

He chuckled. "I'm afraid Grant keeps me well supplied with cookies."

"How about a cup of tea?"

"Deal. Your secret is safe with me."

She made two cups of tea and brought them to the living

room, where Drew was on the floor petting all three dogs. She set his tea on the table nearest him before folding herself into the corner of the couch.

"Thank you for today, Drew." She watched as the dogs vied for his attention. "The sleigh ride was unforgettable. Jake will cherish the memory of it forever."

"It was a fun day for me, too. I haven't done that in years. Milt, he's the driver and owner, always invites me each year. I take care of his horses and other animals. I just never felt like doing it until this year."

"It was a perfect day."

Sunday morning, Hope crept out of bed early, praying Jake would stay asleep. As she made a cup of tea, she peered out the windows and saw mounds of beautiful snow on the ground and bushes. Jake would be thrilled.

After turning the Christmas tree lights on, she snuggled into the leather chair with her tablet. The morning hours, when it was still dark, and the house was asleep, were her favorite times. Always had been.

She opened her tablet and found Tina's social media account. She scrolled through the posts. Selfies of her daughter alone and with friends dominated the feed. Tina was having fun and enjoying college. No mention of her family or the drama surrounding it.

Hope hated the idea of her daughter's posts being so public. At the same time, she was thankful her daughter was too naïve or couldn't be bothered to lock down her account and keep things private. It was her only window into her daughter's existence.

The desire to send Tina a note or a message was overwhelming, but she resisted. She couldn't risk the chance of

Brian finding her and knew Tina's loyalties didn't lie with her.

After reading the news and touching her finger to her daughter's face one more time, she began prepping for breakfast. Once she got the egg dish baking, she hurried back to the bedroom for a quick shower and changed into warm clothes. Jake was still asleep when she tiptoed down the hallway.

The first guests began milling around in search of coffee before eight o'clock. While she chatted with the guests, she made waffles to go with the egg bake. The delicious aroma coming from the kitchen enticed the rest of the guests to the dining room.

Jake, trailed by Scout, wandered into the kitchen as the others were eating. He got his first glimpse of snow at the backdoor. "Mommy, Mommy. Look, look. Lots of snow. We have to call Drew."

She fixed Jake a plate and hoisted him into a chair at the counter. "He'll be here soon. I'm sure he noticed the snow at his house."

Jake shoveled in his breakfast and took off to get changed. While he was getting ready, Drew and his dogs arrived. He confined them, along with Scout, to the mudroom and came into the kitchen.

"I see my timing is impeccable." He grinned and took the warm waffle Hope offered, adding a generous helping of the egg and sausage casserole. Noticing the remnants of Jake's breakfast, he added, "I'm sure Jake is stoked about the snow."

Hope smiled. "Yes, he's getting ready right now. He wanted to call you."

The sound of Dottie's walker clicking on the hardwood announced her entrance to the kitchen. Hope fixed her a plate and Drew helped her into Jake's abandoned chair. "The snow is beautiful this morning," she said, wrapping her hands around the warm cup of coffee Drew had fetched.

"I promised Jake we could build snowmen today." He asked for a second waffle. "I'm going to need extra energy to keep up with that guy today." Dottie reminded him to retrieve the bin of accessories for the snowmen from her stash of decorations in the closet.

The guests were slow to leave, lingering over coffee and visiting with Dottie. Hope took advantage of the lull in her cleaning activities and watched the snowmen making from the porch.

A sliver of sunlight peeked through the clouded sky, causing the snow in the yard and trees to sparkle like glitter. She laughed at the dogs who romped across the yard, their noses building tunnels and creating soft piles of snow. Drew showed Jake how to roll balls of snow across the lawn to make the huge bodies of the snowmen.

Amid the building, Jake and Drew got in a few snowball fights. Listening to the unabandoned laughter of her son and watching the bond between the two strengthen, Hope wondered how she would ever be able to leave Silver Falls.

13

After the guests left Monday morning, Hope worked all day to get the laundry done and the rooms ready for the weekend. In between loads of laundry and bedmaking, she checked on Jake and made sure his schoolwork was done.

He had been intrigued with the horses pulling the sleigh and chose to do a report on horses. "I'm going to ask Drew all about horses. Maybe he can take me to see more of them if he has any sick ones."

"Don't bug him. Write down all your questions, and then you can give them to him. I'm sure he's tired after work and doesn't need you bombarding him."

He set out with his notebook and began printing out his queries. Dottie let Hope use her computer to print some age-appropriate information about horses. She also found some sheets of horses for Jake to color.

This weekend, with Christmas only a week away, it was the grand finale of the festival. There were contests scheduled all weekend. Competitions included gingerbread houses, ice sculptures, ugly sweaters, bingo games, and a candy cane hunt.

A fireworks display planned for Saturday night would be the highlight of the weekend. A snowman building contest was also on the schedule, providing there was a supply of snow.

The guesthouse was booked solid, meaning Hope would have to give up the Blue Room and move into the spare room next to Dottie on Friday. No guests were expected until Thursday, so she had a few days to spend helping Grant at the bakery.

On Wednesday, when she finished at the bakery, she stopped by Chet's garage. Amy looked up from the counter and smiled. "Hello, Hope. How are you?"

"Terrific. Just stopped by to check on my account and see how close I am to having enough for Chet to order the parts."

Amy tapped some keys on her keyboard. "It looks like you have just over twenty-five hundred dollars credited to your account, so you're close."

Hope shook her head. "That can't be right. I haven't worked enough hours for that much."

"Oh, there's been a few donations." Amy grinned.

Hope shook her head. "Grant?"

The woman held up her hand. "I'm sworn to secrecy about the particulars," said Amy. "The donations came from lots of people in town. Not Grant."

"What do you mean?"

"Silver Falls is a close-knit community. We like to help people. Chet's told a few people about your predicament, and lots of people want to help. They stop by and put a few dollars on your account. That's all. Just being neighborly."

Hope's voice caught, and tears filled her eyes. "You mean total strangers donated to help me?"

"That's right." She handed Hope a tissue. "Silver Falls has a lot of holiday spirit. It makes people feel good to help someone who needs it."

Hope nodded. "Thank you, Amy. Please thank Chet for me. I'm more than surprised." She turned to leave and added, "Tell Chet to go ahead and order the parts when there's enough money. There will be more added at the end of the week from the bakery."

With a grateful heart, Hope traversed the streets, lined with clumps of dirty snow, back to the guesthouse. Dottie and Jake were in the kitchen enjoying a cookie break.

Hope kissed the top of his head and plucked one of the cookies from the plate. "Did you get your schoolwork done?"

Jake nodded. "We just finished it all." He finished his cookie and scampered off with Scout.

Dottie nodded and turned her eyes to Hope. "You look mighty happy, dear. What's got you smiling?"

She explained what she had discovered at Chet's. "I'm overwhelmed at the kindness in Silver Falls. I never dreamed people would be so generous."

Dottie smiled and patted her hand. "It's the way we do things here. It's why I love living in this beautiful place." She lowered her voice and added, "The only downside is it means you'll be leaving sooner than I wanted."

Friday morning Hope moved all her things into the boys' old room. Jake loved having his own twin bed and saw no downside to the change in location. Hope got the Blue Room ready for guests and spent the day making sure she had everything she needed to make breakfasts for the weekend.

The anticipation for tomorrow's activities and the fireworks had kept Jake on his best behavior all week. His schoolwork, including his draft report on horses and some extra pages he was completing so he could have a break over Christmas, had been turned in Friday afternoon.

Drew promised him a trip to a horse farm after Christmas, and he was counting the days. Hope wrestled with ideas for a Christmas gift for Jake. She couldn't afford much but wanted to make sure he had something special under the tree. She had been saving her portion of the tips from the bakery to buy gifts. She hoped to be able to buy Dottie, Drew, and Grant something to show her appreciation for all they had done.

All the guests arrived at once on Friday afternoon. As soon as she got the last couple settled, she checked the time and found it well after five o'clock.

Drew was in charge of dinner Friday night and that meant takeout. He arrived with apologies for being late and bags from his favorite Chinese restaurant. Grant followed with leftover cupcakes from the bakery. Hope helped set the table, and they dug into the spread.

Plans for Saturday dominated the conversation. Hope reminded Jake she wouldn't be able to get an early start. She had to make sure all the rooms were straightened and the chores done. Jake's bottom lip protruded in a dramatic pout.

Drew said, "I don't mind taking Jake. You could join us later in the day or take some time for yourself."

"Are you sure?" She didn't want to burden Drew with a sure to be sugar-laden seven-year-old. "He can be a handful." She gave her son an admonishing look.

"I'll be good. I promise. Pleeease, Mommy."

"On one condition." She narrowed her eyes and said, "If you give Drew one bit of trouble, he is to pack you up and bring you back here. That means no fireworks for you unless you behave."

He stopped eating his cupcake and nodded as she spoke.

At her comment about the fireworks, his eyes went wide. "I promise. I'll be extra good."

Drew ruffled the boy's thick, dark hair. "We'll be fine. Don't worry."

"Finish up your cupcake and then it's time for bed. You need to get a good night's rest if you want to go with Drew tomorrow."

He ate the last bite and helped clear the table before giving his mom a kiss. He hugged the other three, lingering longer when he embraced Drew. Hope saw him whisper something in Drew's ear and watched both of them smile.

Grant helped Dottie to the living room before he called for his dogs. "See you guys tomorrow at the festival," he said, bundling into his coat and making his way outside.

Hope checked Jake's toothbrushing and tucked him into his bed with Scout next to him. "Sleep tight, little buddy. Love you lots." She kissed his forehead, gave the dog a scratch behind his ears, and shut the door, leaving the night-light on to help guide her when she retired for the evening.

Drew dawdled in the kitchen while Hope did the dishes and made another breakfast dish for the morning. In a low voice, Drew said, "I heard from Mark today, and he has an update for you."

She signaled with her eyes toward the living room. "Let's wait until your mom goes to bed."

As she finished cleaning up the mess she made with the casserole, Dottie called out, "I'm going to call it a night. See you two in the morning."

Drew followed her down the hall, to her wing of the house. Hope made two cups of tea and waited for Drew to return. After several minutes, he joined her at the counter.

She gave him a questioning look. "So, what's the update?"

"I hate to be the one to tell you all this. Mark said you can call him directly if you prefer."

She shook her head. "No, go ahead. It's fine. You know my whole story. I don't have anything to hide."

He sucked in a breath. "He found out Brian is involved with a woman. A younger woman from his office. That's the bad news."

The color drained from her face, but she remained stoic. "So, there's some good news?"

"Brian filed for divorce in absentia in Illinois. He did that right after you left in early September." He went on to explain the process, as Mark had educated him earlier in the day. "Brian can file alone as a resident of Illinois and since he doesn't know your whereabouts, a notice is printed in the newspaper for a certain period of time. This satisfies the requirement that you be notified."

She listened as he clarified various points and timelines. "Bottom line, Mark is sure he could negotiate with Brian's attorney to have the divorce granted in Nevada since it has such a short residency requirement. The proceedings in Illinois will take longer, and it seems Brian is anxious to remarry."

She sipped her tea and swallowed. "What about Jake?"

"Mark said in the filings in Illinois he was willing to give you full custody. He plans to ask for child support and some type of monetary settlement for you. He's convinced Brian will agree once he knows Mark will use the photos you kept."

Tears fell onto her cheeks. She wiped them with the back of her hand. "Sorry, I'm relieved but sad. I understand he's done with me, but Jake has done nothing." She held up her hand and said, "Don't get me wrong, it beats a long custody battle, but how do I explain his daddy doesn't want him anymore?"

He reached for her hand and held it in his. "I don't have a good answer for that one." He muttered something uncomplimentary under his breath.

She cracked a smile. "My thoughts exactly."

"So, do you want to talk to Mark and tell him to proceed with the filing. He reviewed your arrival here and said we can use this as your residence. To meet the legal requirement, it means filing on Christmas Eve."

She nodded. "Yes, I want this to be over."

Drew pulled his cell phone from his pocket. "He said to call him tonight, no matter the time." He scrolled through to Mark's name. "He said he would meet you on Sunday to sign the paperwork. I can run you over to his office."

She took the phone. He stood and made to leave. She grabbed his arm and said, "Please stay. I couldn't have done this without you."

After Dottie read the paper Saturday morning, she left it to be recycled. The guests got an early start and Drew had picked up Jake a few minutes later. Dottie was in her room, and Hope had the house to herself.

After she put together the ingredients for chili and set the slow cooker, she selected one of the fresh almond croissants Grant had delivered, refilled her tea, and grabbed the newspaper.

The middle of the paper was full of Christmas advertisements and sales. She spied some possible options and tore out the coupons and put them in her purse. After she got the rooms straightened and replenished, she tossed the towels in the washer and checked on Dottie.

She made them a snack and visited until it was time to transfer the laundry to the dryer. "I'm going to take off," she hollered down the hallway. "If you need anything, just call one of us. We'll be home for dinner before the fireworks."

Hope set out in Dottie's car and chose to leave the car at City Hall, a few blocks from her destination. She found the first store on her list. After a bit of browsing, she found the perfect gift for Jake. It was on sale, and the coupon saved her a few more dollars. They even wrapped it for her.

Next, she hit a store down the street. She had a hard time deciding, but the helpful clerk weighed in, helping her select gifts for Drew, Dottie, and Grant. They weren't much, but they conveyed the special place each of them held in her heart. She had money left from her tips and bought Jake a new pair of pajamas he could open on Christmas Eve.

She searched for a new game and after combing the shelves found one that was in her price range and looked fun. The balance of her money went to stocking stuffers she knew Jake would enjoy. She added those to her bag of gifts and hurried to the car. After stashing the presents in the trunk, she drove to the bakery and parked in one of the reserved spots.

Drew and Jake weren't there, but Grant suggested she might find them at the outdoor ice-skating rink they built for the festival. She took a chai tea latte to go and set out on her search.

The town was bustling with activities. She passed by the rows of gingerbread houses that had been judged and saw several people in Christmas sweaters that were beyond gaudy. The outdoor rink was teeming with skaters of all ages. She scanned the area and spotted Jake, holding onto Drew's hand. They were gliding along, both grinning and laughing.

Not wanting to break their concentration, she watched from behind a crowd. As the sky darkened, people began leaving the ice. Jake and Drew finished a few more laps and then skated to the edge. She watched as Drew helped Jake remove his skates and tied his shoes. He handed the boy an oversized stuffed dog wearing a Santa hat.

She met them at the exit and said, "I can't believe you were skating, Jake. You did so well." She turned to Drew. "He's never skated. I can't believe you talked him into it."

"It was sooo much fun. I fell a few times but Drew caught me, and it didn't hurt."

"Looks like you had a great time, buddy." She took his gloved hand in hers. "So, tell me about your doggie friend."

"We won it at bingo. His name is Buster." He rambled on about watching the ice sculpting contest and told her his favorite was a reindeer.

Drew pulled two handfuls of candy canes from his coat pockets. "We did well in the candy cane hunt, too."

"And we had hot dogs and hot chocolate for lunch." Jake hugged the stuffed dog to his chest. "It was the best day ever."

"I've got chili cooking. Are you guys ready to head home and have dinner before the fireworks? Dottie will want to hear about all your adventures."

He skipped his way down the street, a few steps in front of them. "I hope he wasn't too much trouble. I can see he had a wonderful time," said Hope.

"It was a great day. Like he said, the best day ever. The best day I've had in years." Drew's smile did little to hide the sadness in his eyes.

"I'm sure this hasn't been easy for you. Having Jake around. I'm sure it reminds you…"

He shrugged. "Sometimes it hits me, and I think of all I missed with Danny."

She grabbed his hand. "I'm sorry, Drew. I can't imagine it."

"Jake's laughter and happiness are the perfect cure. We lived like dogs today. In the moment."

After bowls of chili with Grant's fresh from the oven corn-bread, they all piled into Drew's SUV and drove downtown. He cruised the residential streets surrounding Maine Street and parked in front of a beautiful brick home decked out for the holidays. They had a perfect view of the tree in the center of town just across the street.

"Won't we get in trouble for parking here?" asked Hope, pointing at the sign warning of parking for residents only.

"They're clients and told me I could park here for the display tonight." He turned to his mother, in the front seat. "I figured you'd be more comfortable just sitting here than trying to find a good place to stand outside."

She nodded. "You're right. I love the fireworks, but was dreading standing in the cold."

Jake perched on the center console between Dottie and Drew, anxious for the show to start. Minutes later, they heard and felt the thud of the first launch.

Hope watched with wonder as her son pointed at the dark blue heavens above the tree. Brilliant reds and greens burst forth, illuminating the sky. Hope stepped outside and captured several photos on her phone. Starbursts exploded and then blinked and twinkled as the colors scattered and disappeared.

The show went on for twenty minutes and ended with a grand finale. Dozens of launches flew into the air and exploded in a cascade of colors. Beautiful gold and silver stars erupted and floated on the inky canvas. They lit up downtown like it was daylight and then fizzled and faded as the scattering of colors fell back to the ground.

On the way home, she focused on the stars littered across the clear night sky. She imagined Tina, somewhere in

Chicago, looking up at the same blanket of twinkling lights. She only hoped her daughter knew how much she loved and missed her.

She would contact her and try to make amends, as soon as this whole divorce mess was settled.

14

Drew picked Hope up early Sunday morning. She told Jake she was doing some secret Christmas errands. Grant offered to stay with Dottie and keep an eye on things.

Traffic was light, and the trip to Mark's office took just over an hour. Hope took an immediate liking to the tall man with a crooked smile. He was confident and calm. Mark explained the process again, confirming what Drew had related. He anticipated being able to schedule a hearing the week after Christmas unless there was an unforeseen issue.

When Hope and Mark emerged from his office, Drew chatted with him for a few minutes. "I'll be in touch," Mark promised, as the two made their way out the door.

"I can't believe he's doing this for free," said Hope.

"We go way back, and he owes me a few. I'm starving. What do you say we stop for a quick bite?" He described a family restaurant he always enjoyed and drove there.

After stuffing themselves with a delicious meal, and Drew refusing Hope's offer to buy, he steered the SUV for Silver Falls. Traffic had picked up with skiers on their way to the snowy slopes.

With two couples having checked out that morning, Hope was able to reclaim the Blue Room. She spent the rest of the afternoon cleaning and getting organized for the week. By Monday, the others had gone, leaving her until Thursday to log more hours at the bakery.

Monday afternoon she helped Dottie make shopping lists for the holiday meals she was planning. "I always make a big dinner on Christmas Eve and another one on Christmas Day." She shook her head as she flipped the pages in her planning book. "I can't expect the boys to do that much cooking."

"Maybe we could do something easy on Christmas Eve and do the big meal on Christmas Day," suggested Hope.

Dottie frowned but didn't discount the notion. She scribbled notes on a tablet. "How about we do lasagna for Christmas Eve. It's a dish we can do ahead of time. We can bake a ham with all the trimmings for Christmas Day. That should keep things simpler than usual."

Hope nodded. "Sounds great. Grant can bring us his yummy bread, and we can add a veggie or salad. That's all we need for Friday night."

They discussed side dishes for Christmas Day and finished the list. Instead of her usual three or four pies, Dottie cut it back to one slab pie instead. After the planning was out of the way, Hope asked if she could use some of Dottie's wrapping paper and ribbon to wrap a few things.

Dottie told her where she could find what she needed in the hall closet and offered to keep Jake occupied. Hope relished wrapping and decorating gifts. It had always been one of her favorite things to do. She missed the large room in the house where she had organized all her supplies and had room to store all her holiday decorations.

She slipped all of her packages behind the tree, hidden

from prying eyes. She had volunteered to cook dinner tonight and was making one of Jake's favorites—tacos.

As she chopped veggies and added seasonings to the meat, the familiar aroma filled the kitchen.

Tears dotted Hope's cheeks as she remembered tacos were also Tina's favorite meal.

Friday morning Hope's cell phone rang, and she saw Mark's number. She hurried to her room to answer. "Just wanted to let you know, we filed the paperwork first thing this morning, and I contacted Brian's lawyer in Chicago. He was a bit prickly when I mentioned a settlement. Not to worry though, it's a negotiating tactic. I reminded him about the photos documenting Brian's assault on you, and he said he'd get back to me."

She inhaled and tried to calm her racing heart. "I'm willing to give up any money, just so I keep Tyler. I don't want him in the middle of this."

"I know that, but Brian and his lawyer don't, and they don't need to know. I'm sure I'll hear from them by Monday. I've got a hearing date set for Tuesday."

She asked if she had to be at the hearing and he confirmed it wasn't necessary. "Don't worry. Try to enjoy your holidays. This will all be over soon. Have a Merry Christmas."

Hope wished him the same and disconnected, her hands shaking as she hit the button. She shut her eyes and whispered, "I wish this was over." She splashed some water on her face and composed herself before returning to the kitchen.

Jake and Dottie were visiting over pastries and fruit. With it being Christmas Eve, the two couples staying made it clear they wouldn't be having breakfast at the guesthouse since they were spending time with their families. That meant no cooking and easy breakfasts for a few days.

Grant and Drew were both getting off at noon and would be staying the night at Dottie's. Jake couldn't sit still, filled with the excitement of the impending celebration. Under Dottie's watchful eye, Hope started making tonight's lasagna.

She had it done and in the fridge by the time the boys arrived with a huge deli sandwich for lunch. As soon as they were finished, Grant said, "We've got a tradition of making some special treats and delivering them to the residents at the assisted living facility. Do you want to help, Jake?"

Jake sprang from his chair and hurried to Grant. Hope and Dottie watched as Grant and Drew gave instructions to the boy. They were making popcorn balls and Christmas tree brownies.

Grant tied an apron around Jake, so he would match the two brothers. He showed him how to squeeze the icing onto the brownie and add decorative candies as ornaments. Drew popped the popcorn, and Grant handled the hot sticky marshmallow-based glue. He and Drew shaped the balls decorated with red and green chocolate candies.

After the icing hardened on the brownies, Jake helped put them in bags and tie them with ribbons. He did the same with the popcorn balls. Grant placed all the treats in a festive basket. "Go wash up and get your coat, and we'll head over."

Hope offered to stay behind and clean up the mess. Dottie kept her company and sipped a cup of tea. "You did a good job raising your boys," said Hope. "They are both so generous and kind."

Dottie smiled. "They are wonderful men and terrific sons. Curt was a fine man. They remind me of him. He would be very proud of the way they've pitched in around here."

"It's obvious how much they care for you. You have an

amazing family. I can only pray Jake grows up to be a fine man, like your boys."

Their chat was interrupted by the return of the three through the back door. Jake beamed with pride when he told her about their adventure. "The residents love it when short people visit," said Grant.

"We've always made a point of visiting on Christmas Eve. So many of them don't have family nearby, and we enjoy brightening their day," said Dottie.

While Hope slid the lasagna in the oven, Jake explained how they handed out treats and fruit for anybody who couldn't have a sweet treat. He told her about the shiny piano in their living room and the woman who played Christmas songs.

"There was somebody there with a dog who was visiting. The dog's name is Honey, and they all like to pet her." He rambled on as dinner preparations continued.

As they sat down to eat, snow began to fall. "It looks like we're in for a white Christmas," said Dottie.

"That means we can make snowmen again." Jake squealed with excitement.

"First, we go to church in the morning. Then we'll see about the snowmen," said Drew.

Grant insisted on cleaning up the dinner dishes, and everyone retired in front of the fire while they waited. When he finished, he brought in a tray filled with tea and hot apple cider.

Hope watched as Jake's eyes got heavier. "Would you like to open one gift tonight?"

He snapped to attention, put his mug down, and ran to the tree. She retrieved the gift she had moved to the front of the tree earlier in the day. "Here you go."

He ripped off the wrapping and revealed the penguin

pajamas she had found for him. He engulfed her in a long hug.

"Okay, doodlebug, let's get you in your new jammies and get you to bed. Santa won't come until you're asleep."

He hugged the others on his way to the Blue Room. "Merry Christmas, guys," he said, as Hope led the way down the hall.

Early Christmas morning, Hope crept out of bed and into the living room. She unearthed the stocking she had decorated and hung it from the mantle. She repositioned her gifts in front of the tree and settled in with a cup of tea.

Her mind wandered to past Christmases with Brian and Tina. Their celebrations had been filled with extravagant purchases. High-tech electronics, pricey jewelry, the latest toys, and overpriced clothes and accessories were piled under their tree. Amid all the material presents, the magic of the season had been lost.

This year she would start over with Jake. This would be the first year they would focus on the true meaning of Christmas. No more over-indulgence. She liked the idea of visiting a retirement home or a hospital to spread a bit of cheer. Doing something for someone else always made her feel better.

The patter of feet coming down the hall roused her from her musings. "It's Christmas," shouted Jake. Heavier footfalls came from the opposite direction and Drew joined them.

Grant and Dottie followed a few minutes later, and they all settled into seats around the tree. Drew reached for the stocking and handed it to Jake. "Looks like Santa left you some treats in your stocking."

Jake put his arm inside and dug around, removing several

small wrapped packages. He went about opening them, getting more excited with each present. Toy cars, a card game, a mini flashlight, and coloring supplies were strewn across the floor.

Drew passed out more presents and Hope watched as they opened her gifts. Dottie hugged the pillow with Scout's picture. "Oh, I love this, Hope. Thanks so much."

Knowing Grant's passion for cooking and baking, she chose a cutting board personalized with photos of Grant's dogs. He held it up for everyone to see and gave Hope a hug. "It's perfect."

Drew opened his and found a glass paperweight depicting a photo of him with his two dogs in the snow. "Thanks, Hope. I'll keep this on my desk."

Jake opened his gifts, which had multiplied. Dottie, Grant, and Drew had all given him presents. He thanked them all for the books and toys, excited to try the binoculars Drew had given him. Hope was rewarded with a sloppy kiss for her gift of a remote-controlled car.

The doorbell rang and Drew offered to answer it. The dogs were busy chewing on their new bones and balls, ignoring the activity at the front door. A few minutes later, Drew ushered in a woman wearing a gorgeous red coat. Her long dark hair fell out of a white hat.

Hope glanced toward the entry and did a double-take. "Tina," she screamed as she sprang from her chair. "Is it really you?"

Jake ran to follow his mother.

Tina said, "It's me, Mom."

Hope engulfed her in a hug, rocking her back and forth. "How did you find me?"

Jake wrapped his arms around his sister's legs. She bent and picked him up, juggling him on her hip. "I've missed you, Ty." Tears cascaded down the young woman's face.

He tugged on her coat sleeve until she leaned toward him. In a loud whisper, he said, "Mommy and I are playing pretend. You have to call me Jake."

Tina smiled and nodded at her little brother. "Okay, Jake."

"I still don't understand." Hope looked at her daughter, bewildered.

Drew ushered the family into the living room. He introduced Grant and Dottie and then turned to Hope. "I know how much you have been missing Tina. With Mark's help, I reached out to her. She's aware of the, uh, entire situation now. She flew out to spend the holidays with you and surprise you."

Hope grabbed Tina's hand. "I can't believe it. This is the best present I could have ever received."

Grant cleared his throat. "How about we give you guys a little time, and we'll get breakfast started." He helped his mom from her chair, and the three of them went to the kitchen.

Hope hugged both her children, joyful tears spilling from her eyes. "Don't cry, Mommy," said Jake. "It's okay."

The mother and daughter talked, while Jake and the dogs played on the floor. They spoke in hushed tones as they discussed what had happened in the past and about future plans.

Hope did her best to explain to Jake that they weren't going back home. "Daddy and I are getting divorced. That means you'll stay with me and we'll find a new place to live."

"What about Tina and Daddy?" he asked.

"Tina will go back to school and visit us on her breaks," said Hope. "You can visit Daddy when he has time." She wasn't sure but wanted to keep the explanations simple. "Our pretend game is over. We can go back to using our real names now."

The boy wrinkled his nose. "I like being Jake."

Tina laughed and tickled him. "But I love Tyler." He laughed as she kissed him all over his face.

Hope left Tina to visit with the others while she took a shower and changed her clothes. When she returned, a huge feast was spread across the table. Fresh cinnamon rolls, eggs, bacon, potatoes, and fruit made for the perfect Christmas breakfast.

The Fishers welcomed Tina with open arms, as they had her mother and brother. They chatted as if they had known her for years. It was close to noon when Dottie said, "I can't believe we're still in our pajamas."

"How about you guys get ready, and we'll tackle the dishes?" suggested Hope.

Drew was the first to emerge dressed and ready for the rest of the day. Tina and her brother were playing by the Christmas tree, where he was introducing her to all the dogs.

When Hope turned around from hanging up the dish towel, she saw a beautiful box gift wrapped in silver paper with a huge red bow. Drew pushed it closer to her. "For you."

"You shouldn't have. Bringing Tina to me was all I needed. Thank you for that."

"Open it. Go ahead."

She undid the ribbon and slid the paper from the box. When she lifted the lid, she saw it. The snow globe. The one she had wanted from the shop downtown.

"I love it." She frowned and said, "How did you know?"

He smirked and gestured toward the living room. "Little guy about four feet tall."

She turned it on and placed it on the counter. Gazing at the perfect Christmas town, she smiled and met Drew's eyes.

"I know you're in the midst of a lot of stuff right now, but I wanted to ask you if you would consider staying here and making Silver Falls your home?"

Her eyes widened. "You mean…"

"I mean, with me. You and Tyler and Tina, if she wants to. I've missed all this. I've missed having a family. I've fallen in love with you these last few weeks. My mom and Grant love you guys. When everything is settled, and when you're ready, I'd love to marry you."

She gripped his hands across the counter and leaned to meet his lips. "I'd love to be your wife."

He moved around the counter and took her in his arms, kissing her while "Let it Snow" played from the snow globe.

When the song ended, he released her. "I love you, Hope. You and Jake."

"You mean Tyler," she winked. "I guess you can call me Abby, now. I chose Hope because it belonged to my great-great-grandmother, but mostly because of my wish for something good to happen."

He wrapped her in a hug and said, "You and Tyler are the something good that happened to me. You'll always be my Hope."

EPILOGUE

At the urging of readers who enjoyed *A Season for Hope*, Tammy wrote another book in the same gorgeous setting, perfect for readers who enjoy Christmas stories. *The Magic of the Season* is the second book in her Christmas in Silver Falls Series. Along with that Christmas story, she's also written *Christmas in Snow Valley*, a heartwarming small-town story about a woman who returns home to spend Christmas with her sister for the first time in several years.

Tammy loves writing Christmas stories and teamed up with some author friends to write a connected Christmas series centered around a woman who welcomes four foster girls into her home during the holiday season, releasing in 2020.

If you've missed any of Tammy's Christmas stories, you can find them all at Amazon.
A Season for Hope: Christmas in Silver Falls Book 1
The Magic of the Season: Christmas in Silver Falls Book 2

Christmas in Snow Valley: A Hometown Christmas Novella

The connected Christmas series Tammy wrote with four other authors is the SOUL SISTERS AT CEDAR MOUNTAIN LODGE SERIES. You can find all the books at at Amazon:

Book 1: Christmas Sisters – perma-FREE prologue book (releases 9/1/20)
Book 2: Christmas Kisses by Judith Keim
Book 3: Christmas Wishes by Tammy L. Grace
Book 4: Christmas Hope by Violet Howe
Book 5: Christmas Dreams by Ev Bishop
Book 6: Christmas Rings by Tess Thompson

ACKNOWLEDGMENTS

I love Christmas stories and spend many hours watching the Hallmark Christmas Movies each year. The inspiration for this novella came to me during an encounter with a young woman in my hometown right before Thanksgiving. The only thing she and Hope share is that her car broke down and she didn't have the money to fix it, so she stayed in our town for several months. My imagination filled in the rest of the story.

My thanks to my editors, Connie and Jaime, for finding my mistakes and helping me polish A SEASON FOR HOPE. I plan to release this book only in eBook format, since it is a special novella for the holidays. I hope it serves up warm wishes to you, regardless of the season in which you're reading it.

I hope you enjoyed this holiday story and appreciate all of the readers who have taken the time to provide a review on Amazon. These reviews are especially important in promoting future books, so if you enjoy my novels, please consider leaving a positive review. Follow this link to my author page and select a book to leave your review at www.amazon.com/author/tammylgrace. I also encourage you to follow me on Amazon, and you'll be the first to know about new releases.

Remember to visit my website at http://www.tammylgrace.com and join my mailing list for my exclusive group of readers. I've also got a fun Book Buddies Facebook Group. That's the best place to find me and get a chance to participate in my giveaways. Join my Facebook group at https://www.facebook.com/groups/AuthorTammyLGraceBookBuddies/ and keep in touch—I'd love to hear from you.

With warm wishes to you and yours this Christmas,

Tammy

FROM THE AUTHOR

Thank you for reading A SEASON FOR HOPE. If you're a fan of sweet Christmas stories, you'll want to check out THE MAGIC OF THE SEASON, the second book in my Christmas in Silver Falls Series. CHRISTMAS IN SNOW VALLEY is another stand-alone Christmas novella set in a cute small town. I've also written a connected series with five other authors, SOUL SISTERS AT CEDAR MOUNTAIN LODGE, releasing in October of 2020.

If you're a fan of women's fiction, you'll enjoy my HOMETOWN HARBOR SERIES. There are six books in the series, set in the picturesque San Juan Islands in Washington. Be sure and download the free novella, HOMETOWN HARBOR: THE BEGINNING. It's a prequel to FINDING HOME that I know you'll enjoy.

For mystery lovers, I write a series that features a lovable private detective, Coop, and his faithful golden retriever, Gus. If you like whodunits that will keep you guessing until the end, you'll enjoy the COOPER HARRINGTON DETEC-TIVE NOVELS.

The first book, BEACH HAVEN, in my new GLASS

BEACH COTTAGE SERIES is also loved by readers. It is a heartwarming story of a woman's resilience buoyed by the bonds of friendship, an unexpected gift, and the joy she finds in helping others. As with all my books, the furry four-legged characters play a prominent role.

I'm excited about my new releases for Bookouture, writing as Casey Wilson. A DOG'S HOPE and A DOG'S CHANCE are two emotional, but heartwarming books about the connection we have with dogs.

Speaking of dogs, I'd love to send you my exclusive interview with the canine companions in the Hometown Harbor Series as a thank-you for joining my exclusive group of readers. You can sign up here at my website.

MORE BOOKS BY TAMMY L. GRACE

Don't miss the **SOUL SISTERS AT CEDAR MOUNTAIN LODGE**,

a connected Christmas series centered around a woman and the four foster girls she welcomes into her home.

Christmas Sisters, Book 1, by Ev Bishop, Tammy L. Grace, Violet Howe, Judith Keim, & Tess Thompson

Christmas Kisses, Book 2, by Judith Keim

Christmas Wishes, Book 3, by Tammy L. Grace

Christmas Hope, Book 4, by Violet Howe

Christmas Dreams, Book 5, by Ev Bishop

Christmas Rings, Book 6, by Tess Thompson

If you've enjoyed Tammy's work, please consider leaving a quick review on Amazon, Goodreads, or Bookbub. They are so very helpful and essential to authors wishing to market their books. Just a quick sentence is enough! To the readers who have taken the time to leave a review, Tammy sends her heartfelt appreciation.

Tammy would love to connect with readers on social media and her website at www.tammylgrace.com. Remember to subscribe to her mailing list and you'll receive the fun interview she did with the dogs from her Hometown Harbor Series as an exclusive free gift only available to her subscribers. **Subscribe here: https:// wp.me/P9umIy-e**

Connect with Tammy on Facebook and click over and follow Tammy on BookBub and Amazon by clicking the follow buttons on those pages.

ABOUT THE AUTHOR

Tammy L. Grace is a USA Today Bestselling Author of the award-winning Cooper Harrington Detective Novels, the best-selling Hometown Harbor Series, the Glass Beach Cottage Series, and several Christmas novellas. Tammy also writes under the pen name of Casey Wilson and has released *A Dog's Hope* and *A Dog's Chance*, both about the emotional connection we have with dogs. You'll find Tammy online at www.tammylgrace.com where you can join her mailing list and be part of her exclusive group of readers. Connect with Tammy on Facebook, Instagram, or Twitter.

facebook.com/tammylgrace.books

twitter.com/TammyLGrace

instagram.com/authortammylgrace

amazon.com/author/tammylgrace

Made in United States
Orlando, FL
12 November 2023